I'm Not Superwoman

I'm Not Superwoman

Marlon McCaulsky

www.urbanbooks.net

Urban Books, LLC
300 Farmingdale Road, N.Y.-Route 109
Farmingdale, NY 11735

I'm Not Superwoman
Copyright © 2024 Marlon McCaulsky

ISBN 13: 978-1-64556-548-2
EBOOK ISBN: 978-1-64556-552-9

First Trade Paperback Printing February 2024
Printed in the United States of America

10 9 8 7 6 5 4 3 2 1

This is a work of fiction. Any references or similarities to actual events, real people, living or dead, or to real locales are intended to give the novel a sense of reality. Any similarity in other names, characters, places, and incidents is entirely coincidental.

Distributed by Kensington Publishing Corp.
Submit Orders to:
Customer Service
400 Hahn Road
Westminster, MD 21157-4627
Phone: 1-800-733-3000
Fax: 1-800-659-2436

Also by Marlon McCaulsky

The Pink Palace
The Pink Palace 2: Money, Power, & Sex
The Pink Palace 3: Malicious
From Vixen 2 Diva
Born Sinners
Used To Temporary Happiness
Returned
A Dangerous Woman
Real Love
If I Was Your Girlfriend: An Atlanta Tale
My Current Situation: An Atlanta Tale
I Wanna Be Your Lover: An Atlanta Tale via England

Anthologies

Blush
Romance For The Streets
Love & Life
The Freak Files Reloaded
Urban Fantasies 1-4 (eBook)
Bad Girl (eBook)

Films

Returned
Temporary Happiness
No Time For Love (short film)
Annulment (short film)

Dedicated to Breonna Taylor & every Black woman
(especially my wife).

Acknowledgments

This book has been a long journey in the making. I wrote the first draft as a screenplay in 2005. Over the years I would pull it out, read it, and make updates, then put it back in the drawer. When I wrote this book, I didn't have the mindset that this was an ode to the strength of Black women, but subconsciously it was. So often in urban fiction, Black women aren't shown in the most positive light, so hopefully this can reflect the other half.

Cynthia Marie, my editor, I've sung your praises for years, but you went above and beyond with this book. Although I must say, if it weren't for our mutual love of *Grey's Anatomy* as our guide, none of this would be possible. Please unclench your teeth and breathe. I know you hate that show. I appreciate how hard you went in on this book even though I know you held back. Thank you so much.

Damaris India DeJesuss, thank you for allowing me to share a bit of your story. I hope I was able to properly capture your courage. Thank you so much!

Thank you to my agent, Diane Rembert, for making this part of my writing career possible. Thank you for looking out for my best interest. I believe I understand your struggle, and I appreciate you.

Darius Lomax, we finally got you on the cover! It felt like this took forever. I appreciate you coming out and doing the photo shoot when you were not feeling well and killed it! You had so many wonderful pictures it was hard to choose. Thank you.

Acknowledgments

Sheena, you are the love of my life, and none of this is possible without you. When you said this was my best written book to date, it meant the world to me. Thank you, babe.

Priscilla V. Sales, you gave me my first break in the industry. Thank you! To every book club and reviewer who has supported me, Robert White, Geneva "The Pretty Bookaholic," Behind The Pages, Strawberry Style, Ebony Evans, and Tina Smith at EyeCU Reading, Literary Divass Spartanburg, Sistah Girl Reading Club Atlanta, Donna M. Gray Banks, everybody at Urban Books, and all the others, thank you!

Marlon McCaulsky
7/19/2023 7:29PM

Originally from Brooklyn, New York, and raised in St. Petersburg, Florida, Marlon McCaulsky is the author of nine novels, including *The Pink Palace, The Pink Palace II, The Pink Palace 3: Malicious, From Vixen 2 Diva, Used to Temporary Happiness, Born Sinners, Returned, Blush, Real Love, A Dangerous Woman, My Current Situation, I Wanna Be Your Lover*, and *Romance For the Streets*, and a contributing cowriter of the screenplays *Returned, Temporary Happiness, No Time For Love*, and *Annulment* for Creative Genius Films. He lives in Atlanta, Georgia.

www.marlonmccaulsky.com

Chapter One

The Legend of the Strong Black Woman

Nia Scott

Chicago, IL

Traffic was thick as I drove down Chicago Road toward the Chicago Heights Rec Center. I was on my way to pick up my little brother, Sean, who was playing basketball with his friends. My flight back to Atlanta was leaving later that evening, and I wanted to spend my last few hours home with him. I stopped at a red light and heard a horn honk from the car next to me. I glanced over, and there was a guy motioning for me to let my window down. I thought nothing of it. Maybe he needed quick directions, or maybe he was trying to tell me something was going on with my car that I hadn't noticed. So I let my window down.

He smiled, showcasing a full set of gold fronts. If "Shiiid, wassup, shawty" were a person, it would have been him. "I just wanted to tell you that I saw you a block ago, and, girl, you are boo-ti-ful!"

I couldn't believe dude was trying to holla at me in the middle of traffic. I should've known better. "Ah, thanks," I replied politely.

"So wassup wit'cha?" He waited for an answer. Because I didn't give him one, he continued, "Why don't you let me take you out or sump'n? If you were my wummun, I would speril you er'day. Trust me, I got the kind of mon-tey that make all your bills go-a-way. Gimme yo numba. I promise it will be the best decision you make awl day." He beamed at his lyrical prowess.

I glanced up at the light, hoping it would turn green, but the damn thing seemed like it was stuck on red, forc-ing me to answer him. "I'm sorry. I have a boyfriend." I thought that would shut down the conversation. Silly me.

"What'cha man got ta do wit' me?"

His response caught me off guard. "I guess nothing, but I'm not interested."

The light finally turned green, and when I started to pull off, I heard my admirer yell at me, "Black bitch!"

Just like that, I went from being beautiful to a Black bitch in the blink of an eye. I earned that disrespect because I didn't want to talk to him? Crazy, isn't it? The last person who should ever disrespect a Black woman is a Black man, but it seems like that's the most common source.

The perception of the "strong Black woman" has be-come a cliché. The idea of African American women as eternally tough and stupendously indestructible is a thing we've been trying to live up to forever. The "strong Black woman" narrative is empowering yet distressing. It's fulfilling yet leaves a part of us yearning for more. Black women are reared to believe that we have super-woman attributes, but what are they really? The power to take on the weight of the world and not break? The ability to break yet hold it all together with a smile on our faces and heads held high? Being a superwoman is a stereotype that has been drilled into my psyche since I was old enough to talk. It's an unrealistic mentality we're forced to take on to survive in this culture, which often leads to us being perceived as cold-hearted, brash, or independent women who don't need a man. When we stand our ground, we're perceived as angry, unstable, and uncooperative. We're the less-cared-about people in America. You know what? I'm not superwoman and don't want to be. I'm human, and I have feelings like everyone else. I hurt like everyone else. I bleed like everyone else, but because I'm a Black woman, that's supposed to make things different. We're marginalized and the most unprotected. We're the group who can go missing and no one worries or even notices. Social paradoxes create a deadly environment that is damned if you do, damned if you don't for Black women across the diaspora. Should I be strong and do everything on my own, or should I let a man take his historical place as a provider and lead? I wasn't trying to be taken care of by any man, and I was damn sure not going to let him lead me anywhere.

The idea of a man being a provider and head of the household was what historically held Black families together. Now the systemic lack of a strong, balanced Black male in what was regarded a very highly respected place is the same thing that is killing our women.

So instead, what do we usually get? We get the most backhanded compliments like "You're so pretty for a black girl" or "You're so pretty for what you are" and it's assumed we're mixed with something. On behalf of all Black women who have received those lame compliments, fuck you.

It's unfair.

Why did I have to pretend to be confident and self-assured at times when I wasn't sure if I was making the right choices? It was hard enough trying to live up to my own dreams, let alone trying to live up to someone else's impossible standards. I was tired of it.

Since I was 9 years old, I wanted to be a doctor. I remembered when I got my first stethoscope. It was a birthday gift from my dad. He told me if I wanted to be a doctor, I could achieve that. I could achieve anything I wanted. And I believed him. That was why I had always been close to my dad. You could say I was a daddy's girl. The day he and my mom split, I took it very hard, almost as hard as Sean.

My father assured us that he was still going to be an active part of our lives. Even though he was busy running his own tech venture, he kept his word. My dad supported us 100 percent. As a result, I received a full ride to Clark Atlanta University, where I was almost done with my pre-med classes and eagerly awaiting to start med school.

Finally arriving at the rec center, I parked and went inside to find Sean. Not that I'm bragging, but my little brother got skills. He was only 15, but he could ball. We inherited our height from our father. At five foot nine, I was above average for a woman. As a kid I was tall and awkward. The boys called me giraffe girl and joked I was Geoffrey's little sister. When puberty hit, I literally went from bony to bombshell overnight, and then them same little snot-nosed boys all of a sudden wanted to be my friend. The same transformation happened to my brother, minus the ass and breasts. His six-foot-four body developed broad shoulders and muscular arms. A well-defined six-pack, natural athletic prowess, and being a starting forward on his high school team made me proud. *Damn, I'm going to miss him.*

"All right, Nia," he called out when he saw me, then yelled to his friends, "I'll holla at y'all later."

"Yo, that's you right there?" I heard one of his friends ask.

"Nah, man, that's my sister."

"Damn."

Sean jogged off the court toward me, and we walked to the truck.

"Your game keeps on getting better. Pretty soon you gonna be ballin' with LeBron and Curry."

"Yeah!" He beamed. "You know how I get down."

Once we got into the truck and drove off, I noticed Sean looking a little sad. We didn't have the typical brother-and-sister relationship. I was more of a mother figure to him because of our seven-year age gap. Especially after our parents divorced. Whenever he had a problem, I was the first one he turned to for help.

"Hey, what's up?"

"Nothing," he mumbled.

"Sean?"

"I'm just gonna miss you." He sighed. "I wish I could go with you."

"You know, I'm going to miss you too. I need you to look after Mom, ya know?"

His jaw tightened. "She's got Leon now."

"Why don't you like him? He seems fine."

A frown painted his face. "That's because you're here. When you leave, he's gonna come at me all sideways and shit like he always does."

"How?"

"He's trying to act like he's Daddy."

"Have you told Mom?"

He folded his arms. "She isn't gonna do anything. You know them hours she be working now. She don't see the way he be doing me."

I'd been home for a few months and noticed that Sean and Leon didn't really speak to each other at all. I just thought it was because our dad wasn't consistent in his life. I never put two and two together until now.

I looked at him. "What does he do?"

"He be trying to stop me from going to practice and be saying slick shit like, 'You know when you turn eighteen, you gonna have to find your own place.' Trying to kick me out of my own house. Man, fuck that dude!"

Sean was pissed. I had to admit I never saw this side of Leon, but if my brother said this was what he was doing, then I believed him. Always.

"Don't worry about it. I'm going to have a word with him when we get back."

"That won't matter, man. Soon as you hit the highway to the airport, he's gonna start tripping again. I'm telling you, he's on his best behavior because you're here."

"Then I'll talk to Mom. I'm not having him come in our home and abuse you. Have you thought about staying with Dad for a while?"

"Nah, he stays too far away, and I'm starting this year. I'm not changing schools because of him."

Leon and my mom started dating each other the year I left for Clark, and he moved in six months ago. Sean had always been honest with me, so I knew he was telling the truth and not exaggerating. It was hard to believe my mom would let any man behave like this toward her son. *Is she really that caught up that she can't see what's going on?* Since I'd been back home, he'd been cool with me, but if he was messing with my brother, I wasn't going to let that shit slide. *Damn, maybe I should've gone to school here.*

Our modest four-bedroom, three-bath, two-story home was in the suburban area of Lake View on the north side of Chicago. My father made sure he moved his family from the more dangerous south side of Chicago when I was a toddler. He didn't want his wife and kids to live in what most people here considered an active war zone. That area was notorious for homicides, more than any other city in America.

My mom came downstairs when she heard us come in. She looked good. Hell, she looked like a slightly older, more conservative version of me. She had a slim frame and golden brown skin. Her long hair was in an updo with gray streaks.

My relationship with her had been strained, to put it mildly, since the divorce. She was a bit old school and felt that I should settle down with my boyfriend, Kyle, and start a family, especially since he was a football star. She eagerly told me to lock him down now before he signed a big NFL contract, but that wasn't even my style. To this day, she never understood how important becoming a doctor was to me.

She smiled. "I was wondering if you were going to get back in time."

"I got plenty of time, Mom. My flight doesn't leave for another six hours."

"Sean, go take a shower and change."

I covered my nose. "Yeah, you stank."

"When I'm in the NBA, y'all gonna love my stank, and guess what I'm gonna say to all my fans?"

My mom sighed. "What?"

"Stank you, stank you, stank you very much!" he sang.

"Boy, you're crazy." Mom and I laughed. She swatted at him. "Go hurry up now."

Leon appeared at the top of the stairs, and the whole mood changed instantly.

"You heard your mother! Hurry up," he snapped, walking slowly down the stairs.

Sean gave Leon that "fuck you" look and walked by him without a word.

"I'm going to put your bags in the truck, Nia."

"Okay, thanks." I nodded and offered a fake smile.

"So I guess I'm not going to see you for another two years?"

"Mom, why you gotta say it like that?"

She sighed. "That's what it feels like sometimes. Besides, you'll find out how it feels when you and Kyle have kids."

I rolled my eyes. "Kyle and I are only dating, and who says I want kids right now, if I want them at all?"

I could tell my last statement shocked her. "How long have you been dating?" She waited for an answer and tapped her foot.

"Two years, but still."

"A good boy like Kyle isn't going to wait for you too long. And there's nothing wrong with having kids and starting a family."

"Wow, that's so 1950s of you to say. Mom, as hard as this may be for you to believe, being a doctor is more important to me than being somebody's wife or mother."

She was taken aback by my words. Truth be told, while my dad encouraged me to chase my dreams of being a doctor, my mother always drilled into me the importance of being a good girl, marrying a successful man, and raising a family. I was raised with conflicting ideas of what I should be as a woman. I could do it all. Was I superwoman?

"I don't know where you came from, but you're not my child."

I pointed to her forehead. "Oh, I'm your child. You see this forehead? That's you. That's all you. Now Sean, that's a different story. That's all Daddy." We both laughed, lightening the mood. There was no denying that truth.

I wanted to talk to her about what Sean and I spoke about earlier, but instead, I went outside to speak to Leon and saw him puffing on a Newport. I was surprised Mom was even with a man who smoked, but I guessed after being married for over twenty years, then all of a sudden being single again, you accepted a few things. He was a medium-built man in his late forties with a chocolate brown complexion and light brown eyes. His head was shaved bald because of his receding hairline, but he managed to keep a neat goatee. He wasn't ugly, but my dad was much more attractive.

"Leon, can I talk to you for second?"

"Sure, what is it?"

"I know you and my mom have been dating for a while, but I've noticed some tension between you and Sean since I've been home. Is everything all right?"

He took a long drag of his Newport, then blew smoke out of the corner of his mouth. I noticed his teeth had a slightly buttery tint to them. *My mother kisses that? Eww!*

"Your brother has gotten a little attitude lately. I guess all teenagers get it about his age, so I had to reel him in a little bit."

"You can feel any way you want, but don't you think telling him he has to move out at eighteen is a little too much? I mean, he's not your responsibility, and you don't have the right to say that."

"Listen, Nia, Sean's a good kid, but he's becoming a man. He needs to stop running up under his mother and take more responsibility."

"Leon, this is his home, and I don't see him running to Mom every two minutes."

"I'm trying to show him a little discipline. She can't hold his hand every time he's got a problem with me," Leon sarcastically replied.

I felt myself becoming annoyed by his attitude. "Does that discipline include stopping him from going to basketball practice?"

"If he doesn't follow the rules in my house, then yes," Leon arrogantly snapped.

My neck craned quickly. "Whoa, your house?"

"Yes, my house," he said confidently. "I'm the man around here."

"Let me clarify some things for you," I said, raising my voice along with my finger. "Last time I checked, this was still my mother's house, and Sean is her son. If ya want to get technical about it, my dad's name is still on the deed. Do you contribute to anything around here?"

My mom walked outside and heard what I said. She darted over to Leon and me as we stared each other down. "What's going on out here?"

"Ask your daughter."

Angrily, he marched inside the house and slammed the door. My mom exhaled, then stared at me. It was like, in that moment, the charade they'd been playing since I'd been home was over.

"Nia, what was that all about?"

"We were talking about Sean."

"What about Sean?"

"Mom"—I folded my arms—"you haven't noticed the tension between those two?"

She shifted in her stance. "Sean is still getting used to Leon being here, so there's going to be a little tension for a while."

"For a while? Mom, it's been six months."

"I know . . . I know. I've talked to him about it."

I cocked my head to the side at her dismissiveness. "Well, Sean's talked to me about it, too. Do you know Leon told him he's got to move out when he turns eighteen?"

She shook her head in disbelief. "Leon wouldn't say that."

I frowned. "He did, Mom. He's even stopped him from going to practice. I know Sean has a smart mouth, but come on. He doesn't need all that. Why are you allowing Leon to treat him like that?"

"Listen, there are other things going on. I love Sean and I love Leon. Neither are perfect, but we're doing our best to work things out as a family."

"A what? Family? Mom, we are your family, me and Sean, and he needs you."

"I'll talk to Leon, but he's in my life now. I need him."

I glared at her for a moment and almost threw up in my mouth when I heard her say that. She really was turning a blind eye to everything, and I didn't like it. For now it was an issue we'd have to discuss later.

Chapter Two

Let's Play House

Nia Scott

Atlanta, GA

The flight from Chicago to Atlanta was quick. I took an Uber and arrived at my apartment near campus and texted Kyle to let him know I was back. My father insisted on paying for my place. He was, in my opinion, overcompensating for breaking up our family. I didn't mind his generosity at all. In fact, I decided to share and pay it forward by extending an invite to an old high school friend from Chicago named Sabina Singh. We'd been roommates since her freshman year. She was so innocent back in high school. Her parents, Akaldeep and Rashi Singh, were originally from Punjab, India, and she was raised as a Sikh.

Like mine, her parents were now divorced. It was a bitter split that left Sabina torn. Her father was very strict, but after the divorce, her mother allowed her to have freedom. Little did I know she would use her newfound freedom to live out her guilty pleasures. I soon found out the quiet girl I once knew was having many sexual awakenings in her bedroom. I had no problem with that. She always respected my wishes along with my personal space. Outside of the occasional rocking of her headboard, I never heard much of anything or ran into anyone she was dealing with. On top of it, she kept the apartment meticulous and cooked some of the most amazing cultural dishes. It was a win-win for both of us.

Sabina came outside to greet me. Her gorgeous long, dark hair was pulled back into a ponytail and bounced with every step. She had a body out of this world as she sashayed toward the Uber, wearing a midriff top with denim booty shorts. I could see why her Instagram was lit whenever she posted a pic. With more curves than a racetrack and a booty that made men rubberneck, she resembled an actress from the old film *Slumdog Millionaire,* Freida Pinto. The Uber driver couldn't take his eyes off her.

"Hey, girl, welcome home," she crooned and gave me a hug.

"Hey, what's up, Sabina? Nice outfit."

"You know me, the Fashion Nova queen. How was Chicago?"

"It was good to see my family, especially my brother, but this is home."

"I know what you mean."

The Uber driver opened the trunk and brought my luggage to me. His eyes stayed focused on Sabina as I took the handle of my suitcase. He looked confused. "I can take it up for you."

"Thanks, I got it from here." There were too many weirdos out here to be inviting them into your home, and with the way he was eyeing Sabina, there was no way I wanted him up in our place.

We walked to the building and took the elevator up to our apartment. Once I got inside, I went to my bedroom, laid my suitcase on the bed, and began to unpack.

Moments later, my phone buzzed. It was a text from Kyle letting me know he was on his way over and his best friend, Brandon, was with him.

"They sent your schedule, and I put it on the kitchen counter with your other mail," Sabina shouted from the living room.

"Thanks." I trudged to the kitchen, opened the envelope, and sighed.

Sabina grabbed a wine cooler out of the fridge. "How does it look?"

"Overwhelming and stressful."

Sabina sat on the couch, grabbed the remote, and turned on the TV.

"By the way, Kyle is on his way over, and his friend Brandon is with him."

She narrowed her eyes at me. "Is he cute?"

"Yeah, he's a sweet guy."

She gave me the side-eye. "Sweet? As in butt ugly but great personality, or sweet as in he has gay tendencies?"

I folded my arms. "Sweet as in he's a nice guy."

"Yeah, right, he probably looks like the Elephant Man, but just in case he's cute, do you want to go to the Gold Room tonight?"

"Nah, I think I want to chill." My mind went back to my mom, Sean, and Leon.

A few minutes later we heard a knock at the door. When I opened it, I saw my baby, Kyle Hicks, and Brandon Griffin. I'm not a superficial type of girl, but Kyle was definitely eye candy. A muscular body wrapped in smooth chocolate skin made him lickable from head to toe. The scent of Burberry cologne was emitted from his body. His eyes scanned over me like a lion eyeing a raw steak.

"Hey, baby," he whispered in a deep, sexy tone and wrapped his strong arms around me.

I held on to him, inhaling his sweet scent. "I've missed you."

"Not as much as I've missed you."

I glanced over Kyle's shoulder. "What's up, Brandon?"

A friendly smile spread across his face. "Chillin'. You good?"

"I am now."

Brandon nodded. He was a handsome brother. He was a tall, well-developed, caramel-skinned man with a fabulous smile. A neatly shaven goatee enhanced that grin of his. I guessed it was true that the fine brothers travel in packs. They walked inside and saw Sabina on the sofa.

"Hey, Brandon, this is my roommate, Sabina."

"Wus up?"

Her eyes lit up. "Hey."

I could tell immediately that she liked what she saw. Unlike some Indian girls, Sabina loved Black men, and Black men loved her. I thought because she was a brown-skinned girl herself, that made her feel comfortable around Black people.

I met Brandon shortly after Kyle and I began dating. They were best friends since high school, and he was the only friend of Kyle's I approved of. He never attempted to flirt with me on the low. He was always respectful and never seemed envious of Kyle's accomplishments on or off the field. *Sabina should be happy to get with him. If I were in her shoes, I would be.*

"Have a seat." Sabina patted the space next to her. "Do you want a beer, Brandon?"

He sat next to her. "No, I'm good."

"What's your major?" she inquired.

"Psychology."

Kyle chortled. "Yeah, you gotta be careful what'cha say around him. He'll analyze shit to death."

Brandon smirked. "I don't analyze anything. I just call things how I see them."

"Shut up."

Sabina slid closer to Brandon, giving him a bird's-eye view of her cleavage. "Are you staying on or off campus?"

"I'm in one of the coed dorms on campus."

"I don't know why you don't stay at the Alpha house," Kyle pointed out.

"Man, you know them fools don't know how to act. I'm going to need to be able to study in peace."

"Is that all you do in your free time?" Sabina asked innocently, twirling her hair.

He gave her a tilted grin. "Nah, I do find time to do other things. How 'bout I show you?"

Sabina grinned. "Sounds like fun."

Well, that didn't take long.

Brandon looked over toward us. "You all wanna go out?"

"Nah." Kyle loosened up the band of his watch. "My knee has been bothering me today. I don't want to be on my feet all night. I have therapy in a couple of days and don't want to hear a lecture about overdoing it."

Kyle was a five-star recruit at the University of Georgia a year ago. Considered a likely first-round pick in the NFL Draft, he was a star running back, finishing as the program's leader in career rushing touchdowns until he suffered a torn ACL. That injury derailed his hopes of making last year's draft. After he had surgery to repair the damage and was told it would be another six to nine months of rehab to return strength and range of motion. Needless to say, he didn't take that news too well, but he'd been diligent about his rehab regimen. The injury put a strain on our relationship, but I supported Kyle the best way I could, and we slowly got back to a good place again.

"Well, why don't you two go and have fun? I want to spend some time with my man."

He smiled. "Can't argue with that. You kids have fun." Brandon looked at Sabina. "I guess it's just you and me."

"Sounds good."

Kyle and I went to my room and lay on top of my bed. I snuggled up next to him and laid my head on his chest. His hand stroked my body, then rested on my ass. His touch felt good. I needed it, and I wanted him.

"Damn, I missed you, girl."

"Hmmm, did you?" I sat up and straddled him. "Why don't you show me how much?"

I pulled my shirt over my head and tossed it to the side. Then I unclasped my bra and let it join my shirt on the floor. His hands caressed my breasts. I pulled off his shirt and kissed him. Our tongues danced with each other, and I could feel his nature rising in his jeans. Our passion was intensifying, desire on overdrive. I eased off him, stood up, and unfastened my jeans. Kyle did the same. Both of our jeans found a spot on the floor near our other clothes.

I grabbed a condom from my dresser, rolled the latex over his manhood, and reassumed my straddle over him. Our naked bodies touched and rubbed against each other. Our breathing became heavier, and I couldn't take it anymore. I slowly eased his erection inside me inch by inch. I moaned and he cursed. Our lips kissed again as I worked my hips round and round, riding his manhood. His arms around my body held me tight as he began to thrust his hips up and down, making me say all kinds of nasty shit. Despite his injury, Kyle rolled over on top of me and continued to stroke me deeper, faster, and harder, enjoying the wetness between my thighs. I bit my bottom lip, enjoying his endless stroke. Soon other positions were assumed, more love was made, and orgasms were had.

By the time we were done, I was more than satisfied. We both fell asleep in each other's arms. Then Kyle, caressing my hair, woke me up.

I gazed at him. "You ready for round two?"

"Damn, baby, I think you're working me out harder than my physical therapist."

"Well, we got lots of time to make up for. I really missed you."

"I'm sure your mom got tired of us being on FaceTime."

"You kidding me? She loves your ass. She keeps dropping hints about getting married and having kids. I can't believe how eager she is."

"Well, your mother knows a good man when she sees one. Maybe we should take things a little further."

"What do you mean?" My heart raced, not knowing exactly what he was trying to say.

"I mean we've been seeing each other for two years, and I wouldn't mind seeing you every day."

"You mean like move in together?" I asked, needing clarity.

"Yeah, I want to be with you."

"But you are with me."

He exhaled and looked at me. "You don't want to do it, do you?"

"I . . . want to be with you too, but I want to finish school before I make a big decision like that."

Kyle didn't respond, but I could feel his disappointment. This was the first time he ever suggested us moving in together. I felt bad hurting his feelings but I wasn't ready to play house yet.

"Are you mad at me?" I asked.

"No. I wanted to know what you thought. Don't worry about it."

Chapter Three

Clark Atlanta University

Nia Scott

My mind was still on the conversation with Kyle. My thoughts on us moving in together hadn't changed. I loved him, but living together would really change the priorities I made for myself. My thoughts were racing as I walked on campus toward my first class.

So many students were moving in different directions. My first year here I felt so lost, like an ant on campus, but after four years it was like second nature. Sitting in my African American studies class with thirty-five other students was normal. After class, as I gathered my things, a familiar voice called my name. I turned around and saw him near the back of the auditorium.

"Hey, Brandon, I didn't know you were in this class too."

"Me either. I didn't even see you down there."

"So what's up?"

We walked out of the auditorium together.

"Nothing much. Just getting used to everything. Gotta head to the Alpha house later."

"You all got something hot for the step show next month?"

"You know it." He grinned. "Maybe a few surprises for you, too."

"I'm looking forward to it. How do you come up with the different steps y'all be doing?"

He grinned mischievously. "It's called Hennessy. Get a cup in me and I let it do what it do."

"You're so stupid." I glanced at him. "Have you seen Kyle?"

"Yeah. He's been kinda moody."

"That's probably my fault."

"Why do you say that?"

I sighed. "He wants us to move in together."

"Oh, wow. I'm guessing you turned him down."

"Yeah, I'm not ready to go there yet. I need to stay focused. I love him, but it's too soon."

"I hear you. That's a big step, and you don't want to do it only to make him happy."

"Right. It's weird that he's never said anything remotely close to that before."

"Well, I guess his injury has made him reconsider some things. Priorities do change, ya know."

"Yeah. Anyway, what's up with you and Sabina?"

He shook his head and let out a chuckle. "Your roommate is off the chain!"

"Oh, Lord. What did she do?"

"So we're up in the club, and ya girl is wildin' out! I'm doing my little two-step, and she's twerking." Brandon showed me how she was dancing by shaking his ass like a stripper. I laughed out loud.

"Yo, she was on one. Then she pulled out her phone and went live on Instagram. I had to draw the line when she wanted to put the flower crown filter on me. I guess after that I couldn't keep up with her, so she started throwing leg to some other dude."

"What? Ugh. I'm so sorry, Brandon."

"Don't worry about it. She's sexy, but I don't think I'm her type."

"Her father was real strict when she was growing up. Kinda like how a preacher's kid gets wild when they get out on their own."

"Ah, it all makes sense now. I used to like them girls gone wild! Boy, I got my first piece of . . ."

He glanced at me and chuckled as if he'd told me too much. I laughed at his crazy ass. I knew he was making a joke out of it all, but I was disappointed Sabina acted a fool.

"Hey, I'll talk to you later. I gotta get to class."

"All right, Nia. Peace."

After my last class of the day, I took an Uber over to Genesis Sports Medicine & Rehabilitation in Camp Creek. I walked in, stood to the side, and watched as Kyle did leg lifts. He was struggling through the pain.

"Kyle, take it easy. You don't want to push yourself so hard. You'll undo all of your progress," the therapist warned.

He always overdid it. Sometimes I didn't know if he was trying to push himself harder or punish himself.

"I'm fine," he hissed.

"No, you're not. That's enough for today."

Kyle slowly let the weight go down and put his head in his hands.

"Are you okay?" his therapist asked, genuinely concerned.

"Yeah, I'm fine. I'll see you in a couple of days."

"Okay, take it easy."

The therapist walked away, and I stood where he was. Kyle glanced up at me.

"Hey."

I gave him a kiss and rubbed his shoulders. "You shouldn't push yourself too hard, baby. You don't want to reinjure yourself."

He rolled his eyes. "I know what I'm doing even if you don't think I do."

I held up my hands. "Whoa, I'm on your side, remember?"

"I'm sorry. I'm just a little frustrated." Kyle threw his towel across the room. "Coach George said I can start working out with the team again and start a few games when I'm cleared. I'm ready to get back on the field. That's my life and really all I know."

"Okay, that's great and all, but if you overdo it, you can hurt yourself even more. Then what? I'm here for you. I just want you to be safe."

He stood up and faced me. "I know and I will be. You want to go back to my place?"

"Yeah, that sounds good."

He looked at me. "Oh, by the way, I got tickets for a comedy show in a couple of days."

"Okay. I hope whoever is performing this time is funny."

"You know, after a few drinks, everything is funny anyway."

We both laughed because that was true. I picked up Kyle's bag, and we walked outside to his car. He pressed a button on the key fob, then stopped in his tracks.

"Damn, I forgot my jacket."

"I'll get it for you."

"Nah, that's all right. I got it."

Kyle walked back toward the building. I got in the car and put his bag in the back seat. I saw the side pocket unzipped and spotted what looked like a prescription bottle. My curiosity got the best of me, and I pulled it out. *A prescription for Vicodin.* It was half empty, but the date on the bottle was four days ago. That was alarming. I quickly put the bottle back in his bag.

Kyle returned with his jacket and got inside. My mind was trying to come up with a rational reason why half a bottle of pills would be gone in four days. Was he really in that much pain?

Chapter Four

Entertaining Guests

Nia Scott

Sweat was dripping down my brow. My heartbeat was strong, but my legs felt like they were on fire. I was burning calories on the treadmill. Over the summer, I pretty much took a break from working out even though there was a gym less than five miles away from my mother's house. I opted to stuff my face with her home cooking instead. As a result, I grew a little belly pudge over the last two months. Even though Kyle didn't seem to mind my little baby fat, I didn't want it to blossom into a full muffin top.

After the gym, I couldn't wait to get out of my clothes and take a shower. I had sweat in places I definitely didn't want it to be. Plus, I needed to read a few chapters and write an outline for a class tomorrow morning. When I walked into the apartment, what I saw and smelled made me stop in my tracks. Sabina and two guys were passing blunts and drinking. There was a cloud of smoke as thick as pea soup floating throughout. There were rolling papers, empty bottles of liquor, and red cups on the coffee table. I couldn't believe what I saw. This was truly some bullshit. Once her eyes focused on me, Sabina gave me a wide smile.

"Hey, friend, I was wondering when you'd get home."

I was speechless and beyond pissed. It took all my will-power not to cuss her ass out.

The two dudes gave me toothy smiles, and then one spoke. "What up, shorty?"

I couldn't believe this dusty-ass Negro had the audacity to say anything to me. I walked by without saying a word to them. "Sabina, let me talk to you for a second."

"All right. I'll be back, y'all." When she rose from the couch, the ugly-ass dude with the dreads grabbed her ass, and she giggled. I noticed that his jeans were unbuttoned and partially unzipped.

"Yo, Sabina, you got some more drink?" he asked.

"Oh, there's a bottle on the counter. Go help yourself." She then turned her attention back to me. Her eyes were glazed and red. "What's up?" The strong smell of liquor and weed-tinged breath filled my nostrils.

"What's up? What the fuck is going on in here? Who the hell are they, and when did you start smoking?"

"Calm down. I met them in West End Mall. I know the cute one with the dreads. He goes to Morehouse. We got to talking and came back here to chill."

"Cute? Came here to chill? That dude don't even know your name. Wake up, Sabina. They came back here to fuck! If I didn't come back when I did, they were going to run a train on yo' ass!"

She rolled her eyes. "It's cool, Nia."

I looked over at them and saw them whispering to one another. "No, it's not. Do you know how dangerous this is?"

"Nia, don't worry about it. They all right and weren't even going to stay long."

An unbelievable urge to slap the shit out of her came over me. If I didn't walk away, she would've caught these hands. I also noticed she didn't answer my question about when she started smoking. *Whatever.*

I went into my room and slammed the door. I exhaled and took a minute to gather myself. Once I found my focus, I grabbed my Molecular Genetics textbook, sat on my bed, and found the chapters I needed to read. Halfway through a less-than-stimulating chapter on the chemical and physical nature of genes controlling development, growth, and physiology, my cell rang, and Kyle's face was on the display.

"What's up, baby?"

"Hey, I'll be there in about an hour, so be ready."

"Ready for what?"

"The comedy show. Remember? I got tickets."

Oh, shit. "I don't think I can go. I got an early class in the morning, and I have to read—"

"Babe, we haven't done anything together since you've been back. You don't want to spend some time with me?"

I could hear the irritation in his voice. I truly wanted to spend time with him, but getting off to a good start in my last year was more important to me than hearing a few jokes. "I'm sorry, Kyle. I really need to do this. Plus, as soon as I got home, Sabina—"

Kyle cut me off. "If you don't wanna go, then say it! You don't have to make excuses!"

"Why are you yelling at me? I'm sorry, but we can still see each other later tonight."

"Whatever, man, I gotta go." He ended the call.

"Kyle? Kyle!" I threw the phone on the bed. I couldn't believe he was acting like this. I sniffed the air, and it smelled like a dead skunk. They were still out there smoking and doing God knows what. My concentration was broken, and I couldn't focus on anything with all this going on around me. All I wanted to do was come home, wash my ass, and study, but with these strange dudes up in here I couldn't take any chances. *Fuck them and Sabina!* My mind drifted back to Kyle's trifling ass. *Fuck him, too. He acts like he don't forget about shit with his selective memory. Well, guess what? I do too!*

Next, I heard music blasting. That was it. I was done. I gathered my books and walked out of my room. I didn't say a word to Sabina. I just walked out of the apartment and slammed the door.

I needed to vent, and there was only one person I could think of who would understand what I was going through, and his dorm was nearby. I decided to head over there to cool off. Minutes later I was knocking on Brandon's door.

"Hey!" he greeted me, surprised to see me.

"Hi. Did I catch you at a bad time?"

"Nah, come in. What's up?"

I exhaled. "So much crap just happened."

"Really? Like what?"

I sat in a chair at his desk. "Well, let's see. I got home from the gym and saw Sabina with a couple dudes in my living room smoking and drinking. She's not even thinking they could rob or rape her and leave her for dead, or me for that matter. Then Kyle called about a comedy show tonight that I totally forgot about. I told him I couldn't go because I needed to study, and he goes off on me."

"Wow." Brandon shook his head.

"I'm sorry. I shouldn't be dumping all this on you."

"It's all right, man. I understand. With everything going on, you can't focus right now." He sniffed. "Plus, you smell like Pepé Le Pew, and I know you can't be happy about that."

I giggled. "I didn't feel comfortable taking a shower with them dudes up in there. I got gym funk and weed smoke coming out of my pores. Ugh."

"I got an idea on how to improve your mood."

"How?"

"Trust me. This will take the stress away." Brandon scrolled through his phone and turned on Stevie Wonder's "I'll Be Loving You Always." "This is what you need."

I heaved a sigh. "I really don't feel like dancing."

"Come on! Do you trust me?" Brandon extended his hand toward me.

I stared at it, then took his hand. We danced. He sang along with the music, and I smiled. The more I moved to the beat, the better I felt.

"Uhhh, oh, yeah. I'm feeling it now!"

He booty bumped me.

"Hey! Watch it!"

"What'cha gonna do about it?"

"Oh, it's like that?" We started battling each other until I couldn't control my laughter. "You're so dumb. I can't believe you got me in here doing this."

He beamed. "Yeah, but you feel better, don't ya?"

"Yeah, I do."

"Now you can focus on your work and deal with the other stuff later."

I nodded. "Yeah, you're right. I needed that."

"That's what I'm here for."

Chapter Five

Roommates

Nia Scott

It had been a few days since Sean and I spoke, so I called him. As the phone rang, I remembered how he cried when I first left home for college, but now after I found out the way Leon had been treating him, I'd been crying. I hated that my mom was letting her relationship turn into a situation like that. He answered his cell on the third ring.

"Ay! Wus up, sis?"

"Hey, little bro, how's everything going?

A heavy sigh came over the line. "Same as usual."

"Has Leon said anything else to you?"

"He doesn't say shit to me, and I don't say shit to him."

"I'll take that as good. How's Mom?"

"She's all right. She's at work right now though. I saw Dad a couple days ago."

"Oh, cool! What's he up to?"

"Nothing much. I guess he's making more of an effort to see me these days."

"I'll give him a call soon. Well, I'm going to go. Remember, if you need me, call."

"All right. Bye."

"Bye." I hung up and felt a little better knowing Sean was okay for the time being.

I started to read again, and then I heard the doorbell. To my surprise it was Kyle. After he hung up on me I wasn't about to be the first one to reach out. We stared at each other for a moment when I opened the door.

"Hey," he timidly greeted me.

"What do you want?"

He sighed. "I know you're mad at me."

"Am I? Really? How could you tell?" I rolled my eyes and crossed my arms.

"I totally overreacted, baby. I'm sorry."

I was so annoyed. The way he spoke to me really bothered me. I let him stand there and sweat before I responded, "Come in."

"I lost my cool, and I know that's no excuse, but I've been so stressed. I was looking forward to seeing you and spending time together. I got in my feelings."

"Kyle, you made me feel like less than shit. You know I'm pre-med. After I took my MCAT before summer break, everything has been going extremely fast. I've had to apply to fifteen different medical schools in hopes of getting accepted into at least two programs. I've had to get letters of recommendation for residency with crazy deadlines, I've been dealing with things at home, and to top it off, my class schedule is ridiculous. I really do want to spend time with you, but you have to be more understanding of what I have going on."

"I know that now, so whatever time you need, you got it."

He walked toward me and put his arms around my waist. I had to admit it felt good to be in his embrace.

"I swear I'll never do you like that again."

"A'ight."

He kissed me softly.

"But if you ever trip like that again, it's going to be an even bigger problem."

"Don't even think like that. Whatever ya wanna do, we'll do."

"How about we go to the Greek step show?"

He nodded. "You got it."

I was such a sucker for him. I should have been ashamed of myself for feeling like this. Just two seconds ago I was pissed off at him, and now I was like a 13-year-old with a crush. I was enjoying this moment so much that I didn't even want to address what was of concern to me.

I had a serious talk with Sabina about what happened and, more so, what could have happened. She seemed to understand and promised to be more considerate. I noticed that every other night she was out and didn't come home, but that was her business. I wasn't her mother and wasn't going to act like it.

Tonight she decided to stay in, and I got her to do my hair for the Greek show tomorrow. We watched videos on YouTube while she braided my hair.

Sabina stared at this one girl with a smile on her face. "I wonder how much they get for each video."

"Not enough for me."

"Why not?"

"Isn't being a video model played out? Most of these chicks make more on OnlyFans doing that, and besides, I'm sure they're asked to do a lot more off camera," I surmised.

"Well, it's their choice if they decide to mess around with the artists. Look at that R&B singer Beata Douglas. I bet she messed with the rappers before she got her record deal."

"I'm not hating on her or any chick, but there's a lot of bullshit that goes along with it. Just be professional and do what you gotta do to secure that bag."

"Shit, if I had the chance to get with Quavo, I would jump on it."

"Girl, you a mess." I cackled. "Anyway, what's up with you and Brandon?" I already knew what happened. I wanted to get her version.

"There is no me and Brandon. He's cute but boring!"

"Really? Boring? I never got that from him."

"Well, he is. When we went out, I ended up having to leave his ass. You know, I'm trying to look cute, do sump'n for the Gram, and he was just standing there watching me. So I ran into Tony, and he got up on it and wouldn't let me out of his sight. We're supposed to hook up tomorrow night."

"Brandon's a laid-back kind of guy, so maybe you were just too much to handle."

"Well, you snooze, you lose," Sabina asserted. Her cell phone started to ring, and she picked up. "Hello? Who this? Darius, why you always playing? I'm braiding my girl's hair now. I'll be done soon. You want to see me tonight? I don't know. I got class in the morning. Why you gotta say it like that? Okay, but just for a minute. All right, I'll see you then." Sabina ended the call.

"Who's Darius?"

"You know, the one who was over here the other day."

"Oh. The ugly one with the short hair, or the uglier one with the dreads?"

Sabina looked at me. "Girl, neither one was ugly. Do you mind if he comes over later? If you do, I'll tell him I'll meet him somewhere."

"That's fine," I sighed. "He can come over."

I appreciated her asking me. It looked like our talk went well. Regardless of what Sabina said though, they were both ugly.

***

Later that night, Darius came over and watched a movie with us. *He isn't as ugly as I thought he was when I first saw him.* He was a tall brown-skinned brother with light brown eyes and a low fade. He wore tight-ass jeans and a bright multicolored shirt.

Darius looked at me. "Sorry about the other day."

"It's all right. I'm over it."

"My homeboy don't know how to act."

So he's going to put it all on his boy like he wasn't doing the same thing. Funny. "It's okay."

"I gotta use the potty. Excuse me."

Sabina got up and went down the hallway to the bathroom. Darius and I sat there for a second in silence, watching the movie. He then stared at me. "What's up with you?"

"Nothing."

"You just be by yourself all the time?"

I looked at him strangely. "Yeah, unless I'm with my man."

He nodded. "It don't look like your man be taking care of you. You don't look happy. You always seem uptight."

"My man takes care of me just fine. Aren't you here with Sabina?"

A stupid grin spread across his face.

I take back what I said earlier. His ass is ugly.

"We cool. I'm asking, what can I do for you?"

I scowled. "Not a goddamn thing."

"Come on, shorty. I know your man ain't hitting that right. I can work that thang out for you. I know your girl done told you about my dick. You see she's always smiling. A dick a day will keep the frowns away."

This fool thinks I'm a ho! I couldn't believe the level of disrespect he was giving me. "Listen very carefully." I pointed my finger at him. "My man got all the dick I need, so keep your funky ass away from me." I got up and walked to my room.

Sabina came out of the bathroom. "Hey, Nia, I was gonna—"

I slammed my door before she finished her sentence.

"What's wrong with her?" I heard her ask Darius.

"I don't know," he lied. "She just got up and left."

The nerve of him! That confirmed that Sabina's taste in men was piss poor. Darius was a pig. An asshole, to be more accurate. *The nerve of that fool trying to get in my pants! Do I got "freak ho" written on my forehead or something?* I would have told Sabina what he suggested, but she probably wouldn't have cared considering she was about to spit on his dick tonight. *What the hell am I going to do about her?*

Chapter Six

My Bad, Pimp

Nia Scott

The Atlanta Civic Center was filled with college students and fraternity and sorority members. A live band was on stage doing a version of "Swag Surfin'," making the crowd rock back and forth. This was why I loved my HBCU. Every day was a celebration of Blackness and embracing of culture. This was the first time Kyle and I went out after our blowup the other day. We spotted Brandon as soon as we walked inside. He was with one of his frat brothers, Jason Trammell, who had a well-documented reputation of getting with as many women as he could. It seemed like most of the guys who were friends with Kyle were like that except for Brandon.

Brandon flashed a smile. "What's up, y'all?"

"What's up, dawg?" Kyle gave Brandon some dap.

"What it do, y'all?" Jason said in a cool, smooth tone and nodded. Brandon gave me a shoulder hug.

"You ready to do this?" I asked.

"We'd better be." He looked at Kyle. "I wish you were stepping with us."

He shrugged. "Well, you know that's how it goes."

"Yeah. Hey, where's ya girl?"

I rolled my eyes. "Sabina said she'll be here, but you know how she gets caught up sometimes."

"Don't I know." Brandon laughed.

Jason's eyebrows rose. "Sabina? That fine Pocahontas-looking girl who be wearing them booty-cutter shorts?"

"You do know she's not Native American. Her family is from India," Brandon clarified.

Jason shrugged. "Same difference."

I rolled my eyes.

Brandon looked at us. "Well, I'll catch up with y'all after the show."

"Good luck!"

"Thanks!"

Brandon and Jason made their way backstage, and we found a couple of seats near the stage. I had been looking forward to seeing the show all week. As we got settled, I was vibing with the band but noticed Kyle had an odd look on his face.

"You and Brandon have become real close, huh?"

I gave him the side-eye. I really didn't like the tone of his question. "We're cool. He doesn't try to flirt with me like some of your other boys."

"Oh, okay." He nodded.

A few minutes later the show began, and the steppers from each fraternity and sorority took the stage and performed their routines. The crowd was hype, damn near doing their own dance along with them. Finally, Alpha Ki Alpha took the stage, did their thing, and the crowd went wild. Brandon was front and center leading the group. I was yelling and stepping myself. They were damn good! The step show came to an end soon after they left the stage.

"Damn, that almost makes me wish I had become a Delta," I told Kyle while we walked outside.

He sneered. "Then I'd never see you."

"I'm sure I would find a way."

Brandon found us in the crowd. He was beaming with excitement as he should have been. They shut the place down. "Sooo . . . what did you think?"

I gave him a fist bump. "Y'all were tight! I knew you was going to come with it!"

"Thanks!" He looked at Kyle.

"It was a'ight."

I whipped my head around. "A'ight? They were the best ones!"

"It was just all right for me. To be honest with you, I thought some of the other houses got y'all."

"Like who?" I asked with annoyance.

"The Ques." He shrugged. "They were tight."

"Yeah, they were, but they do the same thing every year, and you know this."

"So what?" Kyle shrugged his shoulders. "They did it well, and some of the new stuff you did just wasn't doing it for me. I coulda come up with something way better if I weren't hurt."

"What?" I couldn't believe Kyle was saying this in Brandon's face.

To his credit, Brandon didn't seem as upset as I was. He shrugged his shoulders. "Hey, it was our first time showing the new steps, so it might take a while for everybody to catch on, but a lot of people seemed to like it."

"Like it? No, they loved it!"

He smiled. "Thanks, Nia. I'll catch up with y'all later, all right?"

Kyle nodded. "A'ight, dog."

Brandon walked back to his frat brothers, and Kyle started to walk away as if he'd said nothing wrong. I was still in shock at his rudeness.

"That was cold."

"What was?" He turned and looked at me.

"That's your boy and your fraternity, and you just dogged them out."

"He asked my opinion, and I gave it. Am I supposed to lie because he's my boy?"

"No, you're supposed to be a friend. Even if you didn't think they were the best, show them some support."

"Yo, I'm just being real. He knows me and how I do. You ready to go?"

"Yep." I rolled my eyes and marched ahead of him toward the parking lot.

Later that night I was in my bedroom, listening to music. After the way Kyle spoke to Brandon, I wasn't in the mood to spend the night with him. I told him I wasn't feeling well, and he took me home. I was sure he could tell I was annoyed with him, but he didn't seem to care. As I was lying down, my bladder told me it was time to empty it, so I got up and bumbled through the darkness toward the bathroom. Just when I turned the light on, what I saw next almost made me pee on myself, but it surely made me wish I was blind. There was a grown-ass man, butt naked, pissing in the toilet!

I quickly turned my head. "Oh, shit! Who are you?"

"Oh, my bad, pimp. I'm Tony." He flushed the toilet. "Sabina and me were just kicking it. You must be her roommate, right?"

I glanced over at him. "Yeah, uh . . . I'll let you finish."

He went to the sink and washed his hands, not caring to cover himself up.

"That's all right. I'm done."

He casually walked by me, and I noticed the size of his penis. Quickly, I averted my eyes from his huge package. *Dude must be half donkey with a penis that big. Sabina must have the skill level of Thotiumus Prime if she riding that thing all night.*

He gave me a nod. "Nice meeting ya, pimp."

"Uh . . . yeah."

I quickly closed the door and shook my head in disbelief. I growled when I saw piss on the toilet seat. Now I had to clean up after some dusty-ass dude. When I got back to my bedroom, I locked the door. *How the hell is she going to bring some dude in here and be comfortable with him walking around naked like I'm not even here?* In the morning, after Tony left, I had a few choice words for Sabina. Of course, she apologized and said it would never happen again, but that shit shouldn't have happened in the first place. Between Sabina's disrespect for my home, her inconsistent behavior, Darius, and now Tony, I was just about at my breaking point with her.

When I saw Brandon on campus, I told him about my close encounter last night. "I walk into the bathroom and bam! Penis all in my face! Butt-ass naked standing there pissing, and I'm thinking what in the entire fuck!"

"Wow. I remember you mentioning this before. Does she always have guys up in your place?"

"Yep, but this was the first time I've seen any of them naked, let alone in my bathroom. And I'll tell you what, it'd better be the last time. And why the hell do you guys always piss on the toilet seat? Can't y'all aim that thing straight?"

"Well, you know, after you been laying that wood for a minute, the streams get cross—"

"I don't need to know all that."

"You asked," he replied with a pleased look on his face.

"Thank goodness I had on a slip. What if I were naked or something? I don't know what this guy could have done to me."

Brandon looked at me strangely. "Pause. You sleep naked?"

I gave him the side-eye. "That's not the point, perv! The point is I don't want to see any naked men she's fucking. Period."

Brandon was quiet for a second, and just when I thought he was going to say something intelligent to ease my mind, he didn't. "Let me get this right . . . you were just there staring at his dick."

"What? No!"

"Well, you said he was swinging all over the place, so you must have checked it out."

"He was naked! Of course I saw it, but I wasn't staring at it." Okay, so I was lying. I did stare, but that wasn't the point.

Brandon hooted. "But you did look hard at it, so what are we talking about here? Average, above average, or was he like Mandingo?"

"He was above . . . maybe a little bigger. Oh, geesh, why am I even telling you this? You're such a fucking perv!"

"Sabina is gangsta! Maybe I shoulda tried harder to make things happen."

"Whatever! I'm sure you're sliding into somebody's DMs."

"Actually, no, I'm not. I just been chilling." He glanced at me. "Trying to get like you and Kyle."

I paused for a moment, taking in what he said. "I'm not sure you want that."

"Why?"

"I don't know." I sighed. "Everything's been different since I got back from Chicago. We've been fighting more and over stupid shit. Oh, and I'm sorry about how he acted after the step show."

"That's okay, man. I know how he is sometimes."

"No, it's not okay. I was really upset about the way he acted, especially since I know how hard you all practiced."

"Hey, as long as everybody else liked it, I'm cool."

Chapter Seven

Restless Night

Nia Scott

I was tossing and turning in bed. Too bad I was by myself. Even though I loved Kyle, I was still feeling some type of way about his behavior. In hindsight, perhaps having a little hate sex would have been good right about now. I was horny as hell, and it didn't help that I could hear Sabina moaning passionately through the walls. *Damn, Donkey Dick Tony must be tearing her ass up in there again.*

"Aaaaaahhh, oh God . . ."

"Whose pussy is this?"

"Yours! Oh God!"

"Say my name!"

"Tony! Oh, my God!"

This bitch is Punjabi. Shouldn't she be screaming, "Oh, my Allah," instead of God? I was all for handling your business when it was time to get down, but this sexathon had been going on for almost three hours with no intermission. It wouldn't have been so bad if I had been getting some on the regular, but that wasn't the case, and I kept seeing Tony's penis in my head! *How is she getting more sex in my place than I am? Oh God, I have to get outta here!*

I got up, threw on some clothes, and walked out of my room. I stopped in front of Sabina's door. More moans echoed from her room. I shook my head, grabbed my keys, and walked out. I hoped she and Tony dropped dead!

Minutes later, I was at the one place I knew I could get some with no questions asked. I knocked on the door like I was there to collect the rent. The door opened.

"Hey, baby, what's—"

I gave Kyle a passionate kiss and pushed him inside. *Just kiss him, don't talk,* I reminded myself. We always seemed to fuck things up by talking. Kyle wasn't going to ask me a million questions about why I was there or why I was so horny. He was just happy to get some whenever he could. *I swear I'm gonna do everything I imagined Sabina was doing to Tony times ten!* We continued kissing until we reached the couch and fell on it.

"Let me get a condom," Kyle whispered.

I bit my bottom lip. "Yeah, go get it. Hurry up!"

Kyle hurried to his room. I took off my jacket and began to undress. Yeah, I knew it was more romantic if he did it, but I was really not in the mood for the foreplay shit.

I sat down on the couch, and Kyle's cell vibrated underneath my butt, startling me. I grabbed it and put it on the coffee table, but it vibrated again.

"Who is this calling so late?" I mumbled. Next, I heard a faint chime, and curiosity got the best of me.

Brii, with two missed calls and a text, popped up on the screen when I picked up the phone. I opened the text and it read: Call me.

Okay. It must be important, especially at one o'clock in the morning. I did what she asked and called her.

"Hey," a female voice purred once the line connected.

"Who this?" I replied.

There was no answer.

"Who is this?" I asked again, sternly. She hung up. I redialed the number, but this time the line went straight to a generic voicemail.

Kyle finally returned from the bedroom. "Got one," he sang, happily holding a Trojan in his hand.

I knew I shouldn't bring this up now, but it was going to eat away at me if I didn't. "Who's Brii?"

His face dropped. "What?"

"Your phone was blowing up. I thought it was an emergency at this time of morning, so I called the number back. Whoever this Brii is thought it was you, but when she heard my voice, she hung up."

He frowned. "You're going through my phone now?"

"Don't turn this around on me. Who's Brii?"

He rolled his eyes. "I told you who she was a long time ago."

"No, you never did."

"Yeah, I did. Before you went to Chicago for break. You don't remember?"

I folded my arms and shifted my weight from left to right. "How can I remember something that never happened?"

"You trippin'," Kyle mumbled.

"I'm trippin'? Maybe you told someone else, but it definitely wasn't me, so who is she?"

"Why don't you tell me? Looks like you already made up your mind who she is."

"I'm asking you."

"It's Brii, my ex."

"Your ex? Why is she calling you at one o'clock in the morning? Better yet, why is she calling you at all?"

"She called a few weeks ago to see how I was doing. We're just friends. I can have female friends, right?"

Did he really say a few weeks ago, but he swore he told me who she was a long time ago? "You know what, you can have any friend you want, Kyle."

"I ain't fucking her if that's what you're thinking!"

"It didn't cross my mind, but since you brought it up, you must be."

He glared at me. "No, I'm not!"

I nodded. "So if she wanted to fuck, then what?"

He marched toward me and snatched his phone out of my hand. "Listen. I'm not fucking that bitch! The only one I'm fucking is you, all right?"

"Not tonight you're not."

I got up and left. I couldn't prove if he was lying, but his defensive tone told me everything I needed to know.

When I left Kyle's, the last place I wanted to go was back home so I could listen to Sabina and Tony reenact *Monster's Ball.* I was already going through DWS (Dick Withdrawal Syndrome), so I decided to see if Brandon was still up. I needed someone to vent to. I called before I headed his way, and just like I thought, he was up watching TV.

He opened the door. "Come on in."

"Hey, I'm sorry for coming by so late." I began pacing back and forth.

"What's wrong?"

"Kyle and I got into it."

He shook his head. "Again?"

"Yep."

"About what now?"

"Brii."

"Ouch."

I sat down at the table. "I went to Kyle's to get some, but his phone kept going off, so I thought it was an emergency or something. I saw someone named Brii blowing him up, so being his girlfriend, I decided to return her call."

Brandon chuckled. "What did he say?"

"He got all defensive with me. He said he isn't messing with her, but I don't know if I can trust him. Brandon, I know Kyle's your boy, but I need to know if he's fucking around on me. I don't want to be played or mess around and catch some shit."

"Nia, if he's messing around with her again, he didn't tell me."

"That's great. Just perfect."

I couldn't fight the tears welling around the rims of my eyes. I was more pissed than sad. Brandon pulled out his phone and turned on "I Wanna Love You" by Bob Marley. He extended his hand toward me. I looked up into his eyes and took it. Brandon put his arms around my waist, and I laid my head on his chest. We swayed to the music, and I honestly forgot about everything going wrong in my life. I lifted my head, and we gazed at each other. He began to lip sync the words to me. I smiled as he twirled me around and rested his hands on my waist. We moved closer to each other. As I gazed into his eyes, I didn't know what came over me. I placed my hand on his neck, pulled him closer, then kissed him.

Damn my DWS!

Instead of pulling away, Brandon kissed me back, and the passion of the moment took over. He pulled off my jacket, and I slid my hands underneath his shirt, then lifted it over his head. He did the same, leaving me in my black lace bra. My body became alive with sexual excitement. My nipples became firm, my vagina screaming for attention. He unclasped my bra, and it slid down in front of us between our stomachs. My breasts pressed against his chest. We stopped and stared into each other's eyes as if coming out of a lust spell cast on us.

The realization of what we were about to do made us pause. I stepped back and exhaled. I was about to do the same thing I accused Kyle of doing. With his best friend no less. I placed my bra back over my breasts. An awkward silence was in the room as neither one of us knew what to say. I put my shirt and jacket on and left his place.

Chapter Eight

The Day After

Nia Scott

My mind was anywhere but in my African American studies class listening to the lecture. I glanced over and saw Brandon sitting a few seats away from me. He peeked over toward me, and we made eye contact. Guilt was written all over our faces, so I looked away. An hour later the class was finished, and as I was leaving, Brandon walked toward me. I wanted to run the other way like I was in second grade.

With an uneasy look on his face, he said, "Hey, how you doing?"

"I'm fine. You?"

"I'm good. Nia, I don't want it to be weird between us."

"Me either."

"How can we get past this?"

"I don't know."

He scratched the back of his head. "It's my fault. I shouldn't have let it happen."

"You're not the only one responsible."

"Still, I feel like I kinda took advantage of the situation, and I'm sorry."

"Brandon, you didn't do anything I didn't want you to do."

We both looked at one another with delight. Truth be told, I'd always found him attractive. Being angry with Kyle simply gave me an excuse to kiss him.

"I guess I'm more attracted to you than I should be," he admitted.

I blushed. "Guilty."

"What do we do about Kyle? Do we tell him?"

"No. I can't really be all high and mighty and angry with him for being in contact with his ex after what we did, but I don't feel like I need to tell him anything. Do you?"

"No. And what about us? Do we pretend nothing happened?"

"No chance of that happening, huh? We have to be mindful of what our situation is. I guess I'll just have to find a way to put up with you."

He hollered, "Put up with me? A'ight, I'll wait until your next come-to-Jesus moment."

"Shut up." I hit his arm, and we walked off together.

After class I went home. There were no text messages or missed calls from Kyle. I really didn't expect any. That wasn't really his style after we argued. A couple of hours later, my doorbell rang. I knew it was him. Kyle was a face-to-face type of man. I took a deep breath, then opened the door. We stared at each other in silence. I stepped to the side, and he walked in. It was more awkward than anything else.

"Listen, Kyle, I've been thinking about what happened, and I need to know where we stand."

"Okay, real talk. I don't know what Brii really wants, if it's just being friends again or if she wants me, but either way, I'm with you. I'm not going to jeopardize my relationship with you for nobody. So I think the real question here is do you trust me?"

"I want to. It's just the other night . . . I didn't know what to think."

"I know, and that will never happen again."

I was quiet for a moment trying to decide whether I should believe him. A part of me didn't, but then again, I did almost get busy with Brandon last night, so who was I to judge?

"I need to ask you something. Something that's been on my mind."

"You can ask me anything. What is it?"

I took a deep breath and chose my words carefully, hoping to avoid an argument. "Remember when I came to your rehab appointment?"

"Yes."

"When you went back inside to get your jacket, the side pocket of your bag was open. I noticed that your prescription of Vicodin was half gone and you just got it a few days before. What's going on?"

He nodded. "The pain was a little worse than it was normally, so I took a couple of extra pills."

"A couple? Kyle, that's more than a couple. You can't do that. Do you know how dangerous that is? It's a habit-forming drug, and you could become addicted to it."

"I know. I haven't taken any extra since, Dr. Scott," he replied with sarcasm. "You don't have to worry about that though, I promise. I've spoken to my doctor about getting something stronger. So are we good?"

"Yeah, we're good."

Kyle cupped my face with his hands and gave me a kiss on the forehead. I felt like we still had some things to smooth out, but this was a good first step in the right direction.

***

In the morning, I saw Sabina eating at the kitchen table. I went in the fridge and took out a Hot Pocket. I popped it in the microwave and had a seat in front of her. There were some issues I needed to address.

"Sabina."

She nodded in my direction. She looked like she had a hangover. "Hey."

"Don't you have a class today?"

"I dropped my humanities class. It was too early in the morning for me."

"Did you tell your mom?"

"No," she muttered.

"When was the last time you talked to your dad?"

She rolled her eyes. "Mr. Singh? It's been a while, and I'm not trying to, either."

"Sabina, listen, I'm not trying to be all in your business, but you have been partying kinda hard. You might want to slow down a little."

"I'm all right, Nia. You know I'm simply enjoying the whole college experience."

"And the Tony experience."

She giggled. "Yeah, he's a real experience all right."

"I bet. Just make sure he covers his ass when he's here."

"I'm sorry about that. He told me what happened."

I got up and took my Hot Pocket from the microwave. *She's still young and having fun.* I had to remind myself of that sometimes. "Tony is a little older than you, right?"

"Yeah. So?"

"Is he a student?"

"No, he's a personal trainer."

I nodded my head. "I know you're having fun, but I'm saying be careful around him and protect yourself. Don't let him or good sex make you forget about why you're here at school."

"I'll be fine."

I could tell she was becoming annoyed by me trying to give her some advice. Sabina picked up her glass and took a sip.

"What are you drinking?"

"A little E&J. Want some?"

"Eww, don't you think it's too early to be drinking?"

Sabina glared at me. "Why are you giving me the third degree? I'm not the same little nerdy girl you knew in high school. I'm a grown-ass woman, and if I feel like having a drink now, then I'm going to drink."

"I know you're not the same girl you were in high school, but you need to think about what you're doing."

"Nia, you really don't have to worry about me."

She got up and walked out. Truth was, I was very concerned about her. I felt like I was slowly watching her spiral out of control. I wondered if I should call her mom, or would that make the situation worse and push her further away from me? I hoped for her sake she pulled it together before something real bad happened.

Chapter Nine

Hypocritical

Brandon Griffin

Like the lyrics from the old song by Shai, the very first time that I saw Nia's brown eyes I knew right there that she was the one. I couldn't believe I had met a woman who stimulated me on so many levels. I knew it was sacrilegious to be feeling your best friend's lady, but it was the truth. It used to drive me crazy wishing I had met her first, wondering if she felt the same way about me. I never told Nia the truth about what Kyle did the summer she went back to Chicago, but somehow I knew she knew.

When we kissed last night, I wanted to make love to her, but once again, Kyle was my boy, so we stopped. I wondered, if the situation were reversed, would he? I went over to Kyle's place to hang out, and he gave me his version of what happened that night. Of course, I knew what Nia told me was the truth, but I figured I should at least see what kind of spin Kyle was going to put on it.

"Bruh, you're not going to believe what happened last night."

I shrugged. "Tell me."

He grinned. "Yo, Nia came through last night unexpectedly, and she wanted to get busy. So you know we was doing our thing on the couch, and I got up to get a rubber. While I was trying to find one, guess who hits my cell?"

"Who?"

"Brii's ass!"

"Whaaat? That's crazy." I faked being surprised. "What did you do?"

He threw his hands up. "What could I do? Nia picked up the phone and called her back!"

"Dammmn!"

"Yeah, I came out of the room with the rubber, ready to get my ugly on, and bam! Nia's like, 'Who's Brii?' I'm there with my heart pounding, and I'm stuck like Chuck."

"Damn, dawg."

"I figured I'd tell her it's Brii and say we were just talking as friends and ain't shit happening, but nah, Nia wasn't going for it. She starts to flip the shit on me! You know me, my dick's hard and I'm ready to fuck, and I don't want to talk about that shit now. So I blew up and she walked out."

I chuckled and shook my head. "What are you going to do now, King Ding-a-ling?"

He laughed. "First, I gotta call Brii and tell her ass not to text my cell anymore, and then I have to go kiss Nia's ass!"

"You think Nia is going to accept it?"

"Dawg, this is Kyle Hicks you're talking to. 'Poppa been smooth since the days of Underoos.' I never lose."

"Okay, Biggie, let me ask you something. What if Nia crept out and got her freak on with another dude? 'Cause, no offense, we both know you've been dipping out on her for a minute now. Would you think she would be justified in getting a side piece?"

Kyle thought about it for a moment and looked like he was about to say something deep and profound, but instead he answered in his typical manner. "Yeah, she would be within her rights, but I'd have to cut her loose."

"What? Why?"

"Come on, think about it. If you, as a man, get caught cheating on your lady, you have a fifty-fifty chance of her forgiving you and taking you back. You know why?"

I shook my head. "Why?"

"Because women know that men are dogs and that, sometimes, we might go sniff another bitch 'cause that's how we are, but wifey is wifey. If your lady were to fuck another dude, that's disloyalty. Women are more emotional about sex than we are. They got to give themselves emotionally to another man to let him get up inside her. Besides, I couldn't deal with the thought of some other dude being all up in my lady! She'd have to go."

I laughed. "You know that's some really hypocritical shit you just said."

He shrugged his shoulders. "Maybe, but it's the truth."

Chapter Ten

Life Ain't Perfect

Nia Scott

Looking at molecules in my organic chemistry class, I debated if they looked like they belonged to a jellyfish or a spider. This class was commonly known for weeding out pre-med students. To me, this class was less about chemistry and more about the mental fortitude to push through and make it. It laid the groundwork for biochemistry and pharmacology. If you weren't sure if medicine was right for you, this was the time to get out and find a new major. But for me, this was what I wanted and where I excelled.

As I was taking notes on the lecture, my cell started to vibrate. It was a text message from Sean that said, I'm gonna kill him. I got up and walked out of class and called him. He answered on the first ring.

"Nia, I swear I'm gonna kill this muthafucka if he touches me again!"

"What? Again? Sean, what's going on?"

I heard Leon screaming in the background, "You betta clean this goddamn kitchen up now!"

"You better get the fuck away from me!"

"Sean, what's going on? Sean!"

"Nia, I gotta get the fuck outta here, man! I swear to God I'm about to fuck this nigga up!"

"Just get out of the house, Sean!"

I heard Leon bellow, "You little punk! Get off the phone!"

"Sean, where's Mom?"

The line went dead.

"Hello. Hello?"

I redialed the number, but it went straight to voicemail. Then I dialed my mother's number.

"Hello?"

"Mom, you gotta get home now!"

"Nia, what's wrong? Why are you yelling?"

"Mom, something happened at home between Sean and Leon, and they're fighting!"

"Oh, my God! I'll call you back."

Mom hung up, and I was left standing in the hallway feeling helpless. I couldn't go back to class and focus, so I found a bench outside and sat with my phone in my hand, waiting to hear what was happening at home. Recalling what I heard made me sick to my stomach, and tears poured from my eyes. I spotted Brandon walking my way with another guy. He saw me, excused himself, and rushed toward me. I wiped the tears from my eyes and tried to pull myself together.

"Hey, Nia. What's wrong?" He sat down next to me.

"Just mess at home with my family. My little brother and my mom's boyfriend hate each other. He called me while they were going at it."

"That's messed up. What is your mother doing about it?"

"I don't know. I've been trying to tell her there's a problem, but she acts as if it's not a big deal. Now this happens."

"Maybe she doesn't see what you see."

"She knows. She just doesn't want to acknowledge it. What gets me the most is that I'm all the way down here and not there to help my brother."

My cell started to ring again, and I quickly answered it. "Hello, Mom?"

"Hi, Nia."

"Mom, what's going on?"

"Everything is all right now. It was just a big misunderstanding."

"A misunderstanding? What the hell?" It infuriated me that she tried to downplay everything. "Where's Sean?"

"He went over to your dad's."

"Oh, so you kicked your son out of his own home?" I blurted out angrily. "Is Leon gone, too?"

"Nia, everything is fine now."

I was pissed. "Fine? It was just World War Three in there, and now everything is fine?"

"Nia, please! I'm trying to fix things the best way I can!"

"By kicking your son out and keeping Leon there?"

"I did not kick him out! He's just staying the night over there."

"And Leon could have gone somewhere else as well, Mom. You know what, I gotta go. I'll talk to you later." I ended the call, then looked at Brandon. "You see what I mean? Bullshit!"

He nodded. "The only thing you can do now is hope your mom sees the problem and does something about it."

"Yeah, right. I can't trust her to do what's in Sean's best interest."

"Okay, well, you can't sit here and worry yourself to death either. At the end of the day, she's the parent. Not you. It's not your responsibility to fix this problem."

I sighed. Even though he was right, it didn't make me feel better. I called Sean at my dad's house and checked up on him. He was pissed, and I didn't blame him. My dad wanted to go over there and kick Leon's ass, but I talked him down. I couldn't believe my mom took his side again. *Well, I guess some things never change.*

Chapter Eleven

In My Bed

Nia Scott

I spent the afternoon with Kyle. We had a nice lunch at American Deli, then went back to his place to watch a movie. He apologized repeatedly for the whole Brii thing and how he acted, but still, a part of me didn't trust him. He was trying his best to act normally, but he wasn't himself and hadn't been for quite some time now. His mood swings were becoming much more extreme. He needed help, but he wouldn't accept that suggestion from me. I made a mental note to talk to Coach George and see what could be done.

I noticed a couple of empty vodka bottles next to the trashcan in the kitchen. I wondered if he took some Vicodin along with the alcohol. I decided to make him some coffee and make sure he didn't pass out or worse. After a couple hours he seemed to become more composed, but I was concerned about what he was doing to himself. He wanted to have sex, but after the day I had, I wasn't in the mood.

When I got back to my apartment and headed toward the kitchen to get a bottle of water, I heard a moan echoing through the hallway.

"Great." I sighed. "I have to listen to another night of Porn Hub."

I flipped through my mail and walked toward my bedroom. When I opened the door, I saw the unbelievable, and all the air escaped my lungs. Sabina and Tony were having sex on top of my bed. I was stunned for a second and speechless because they hadn't even noticed me in the room. Sabina was ass up, head down, and Tony was going to town. Then the air returned to my lungs, and I let myself be known.

"What the fuck!"

Tony turned his head and saw me. He swiftly pulled his gigantic penis out of Sabina, which looked like an arm in her ass.

"Oh, man . . ." Sabina mumbled. She quickly pulled the top sheet over herself and stood up.

Tony stood there casually, not giving a damn he was naked, then started gathering his clothes off the floor. "Sup, pimp?"

"You're fucking in my bed?"

"It's . . . not what it looks . . . like, Nia." Her speech was slurred.

"It looks like you're fucking in my goddamn bed!"

Tony walked by us. "I'ma let y'all talk."

"Get yo' goddamn ass outta here!" I roared and threw my bottle of water at his head, knocking him off-balance and sending him into the wall. "You betta not bring your black ass over here again!"

I followed him to the front door, then pushed him outside half naked and slammed the door. I walked back to my bedroom and saw Sabina stumbling toward hers. "Where the fuck you think you're going?"

"Nia . . . we . . . just getting. . . were just fooling around, ya know," Sabina slurred incoherently.

A scowl was painted on my face. "Fooling around? You were fucking in my goddamn bed! Who does that?"

Sabina slurred, "Girl, Tony is . . . and you got that big-ass bed . . . well, he was just curious."

"You think this shit is funny?"

She smirked, and I pushed her up against the wall. I wasn't a violent person, but I'd had it with her. All the bullshit going on with my mom and her controlling boyfriend, and now I came home to this?

I stared into her eyes, and her pupils were noticeably larger. She was disoriented, and I let her go. "What did you take?"

"I'm fine."

"You're high as fuck! What are you on? Coke? X? Both? What's your problem, Sabina?"

Then all of a sudden, she blurted out some wild shit. "I don't have a problem. You're the one with the problem!"

"What?

"You wanna fuck Brandon." She giggled. "You can . . . front all you want to, but I see . . . I see how you look at him. The way you . . . you always run to him. Poor Kyle."

"You don't know what you're talking about, and right now, I don't really care what you're on! You got until the end of this week to get you and your shit outta here!"

She shrugged, and I mushed her upside the head, causing her to stumble into her room. I went inside my bedroom and slammed the door. Pacing back and forth, a part of me wanted to kick her ass, but with the condition she was in, she could die if I beat her like I wanted to. The smell of their sex was still in the air. I frowned, getting a nostril full of the pungent odor. I glared at my bed and pulled the fitted sheet off. I was going to have to burn this shit!

***

After last night's events, I didn't see Sabina in the morning. That was a good thing. I still wanted to fight her. With all these distractions going on around me, I needed to refocus my energy on my schoolwork. I went to the library, found my favorite table, and cracked open a book. I started reading and taking notes. After a few minutes I was locked and focused, but then a kiss on the back of my neck startled me.

"What the . . ." I jerked forward, then turned around and saw Kyle. "Don't sneak up on me like that. You scared the shit outta me."

"Sorry, babe." He took my hand. "I need to talk to you for a second."

"What's up?"

"You know Coach George is going to take the coaching job in Gainesville."

"Really? Wow, okay." I was glad he mentioned him because I still needed to talk to him.

"Well, he talked to me and said that he would like me to be an assistant coach for him."

A wide smile spread across my face. "What? That's great!"

"Yeah, so I was thinking maybe you could transfer down to Gainesville next semester."

What the hell did he just say? I stared at him blankly for a moment. "Transfer? Kyle, I don't know if I can do that."

"We can get a place together, and you know you can get in UF."

"That's not what I mean. I like it here. My scholarship is here at Clark. I would have to take out a loan to go to UF. Not to mention moving to Florida. That's not what I have in mind."

"But with my job that would be no problem to pay back."

"Have you paying back my loan? Oh, no, I'm not letting you pay for my education."

"You're my lady and, I hope one day, my future wife, so what's mine is going to be yours too. I can't do this without you. Is this about us living together? I thought by now you would want to be with me," he rambled.

"Kyle, I do want to be with you, but you can't expect me to drop my life here and move to Florida with you overnight. Are you even considering what my goals are and what kind of effect this move would have on me?"

He looked at me as if I were crazy. "This is a once-in-a-lifetime opportunity for me . . . for us. Football is all I know, and to be offered a job like this is unbelievable. I can't pass this up. If you love me, you'll try to make this work."

"If I love you? Are you really giving me an ultimatum? After everything you've been through and I've been by your side, you're going to say that to me? Seriously?"

He mumbled, "No, that's not what I meant. Listen, I need you. You mean everything to me, and I want you by my side."

"Okay." I sighed. "I need time to think about this."

"That's my girl!" He kissed me. "Let's go."

It was as if he didn't hear a word I said. *Does he not care about my goals and what I want to achieve in life?* I gathered my things and walked out with Kyle.

Later that afternoon, I stopped at the supermarket and picked up a few things before I headed home. I couldn't afford to eat fast food every day, and I wasn't going to survive on ramen noodles alone. The one thing I was thankful to my mom for was teaching me how to cook. Making homemade spaghetti was not only easy, but I could stretch it out for a few days.

After I got done cooking, I heard a knock on the door. I went to the living room to answer it and was surprised to see him.

"Hey, what's up?"

"Nothing, come in."

Brandon sniffed the air and sat on the couch. "Something smells good! What's on the menu?"

I folded my arms. "Does this look like Applebee's to you?"

"Well, with your lack of decorating skills, kinda. So where the grub at?"

"Your greedy ass," I mumbled. "I made a little spaghetti for myself."

Brandon got up, went to the stove, and opened the pot. "I knew you had something good up in here. Damn, it smells good." He grabbed a long fork and tried to get some.

I slapped his hand. "Get out of my pot!"

"C'mon, I just wanna taste it."

I cackled out loud. "I've heard that one before, too. Have a seat, and I'll give you a bowl."

"Thanks, and for the record, when I eat something . . . I lick it clean," Brandon clarified.

I laughed to myself and scooped some spaghetti out for him. Since the night we kissed, we'd been a lot more flirty with one another, but we knew better than to cross that line again. I had to admit, I enjoyed it.

"Kyle told me about the job offer. Hell of an opportunity."

I had a seat at the table with him. "Yeah, it is."

"Have you made a decision about what you're going to do?"

I sighed. "Yeah. I can't do it."

"When are you going to tell him?"

"I don't know. I don't know how to tell him. How could he make me choose between him and my future?"

"I know it's crazy, but it's his choice, and he shouldn't put that pressure on you. By the way, are you coming to the frat party tomorrow night?"

"Maybe."

Sabina walked out of her room, right past us, opened the fridge, and grabbed a soda.

"Hey, Sabina," Brandon greeted her.

She looked his way and nodded, but didn't reply. She proceeded back to her room.

Brandon looked at me. "What's wrong with her?"

"I don't got shit to say to her."

"Damn, it's like that?"

"If you get caught fucking in my bed, it's exactly like that."

Brandon's mouth fell open. "Wait, what? She . . . no!"

"Yep. She did."

"In your bed?"

I frowned. "Yep, getting hit from the back like she didn't have a care in the world."

He smiled. "Did she offer you an invite to join in?"

I ignored his statement. "She got two days to get her shit together and bounce. You're about two seconds from getting kicked outta here too!"

He hooted. "Chill, ain't nobody humping around over here!"

"Have I told you lately how much of a jackass you are?"

"You see, that's your problem. You're so angry. If you get a little doggie style in your life, it'll cheer you up too."

"That's it!" I stood up and pushed Brandon out of his seat. "Get ya ass out!"

Still laughing his ass off, he said, "C'mon. I didn't even finish my food!"

"You ol' nasty." I grabbed the Tupperware bowl he was eating from and found the lid. "Here. Take it with you."

"Oh, c'mon."

"Bye." I closed the door and smiled to myself at his dumb ass.

Chapter Twelve

Break

Nia Scott

Music was booming from outside the two story-house in a suburban neighborhood. College students were dancing and smoking on the veranda as I walked up. It felt like the black cookout with Beyoncé's "Before I Let Go" making sorority sisters step in formation to the beat. The air was perfumed with the distinct scent of weed and pheromones as men and women were grinding. I saw a few familiar faces in the crowd, and then I saw Brandon laughing and drinking. He spotted me as well and headed my way to greet me.

"Hey, you made it."

"It's kinda lit in here tonight."

"You know how we do. Go get yourself a drink."

I nodded. "I'll catch you later."

"A'ight."

Once I was inside, my eyes scanned the room looking for Kyle, but he was nowhere in sight. We hadn't been communicating the way we should lately. I was partly to blame for that. Anyway, I got a bottle of Smirnoff Ice and took a few sips before I made my way to the living room. I started to dance, and a random guy began to dance with me. He didn't do the custom "crotch on my ass" move.

He made eye contact and respectfully danced with me. I was enjoying myself and didn't notice Kyle glaring at us. I was in the middle of a dance-off with the brother in front of me. I laughed as we did some classic old-school dance moves like the Cabbage Patch, the Running Man, and the Butterfly. It was fun to let go of my worries and be silly for the moment. Then out of seemingly nowhere Kyle walked up behind the guy. I made eye contact with him, but he seemed pissed. I noticed the beer bottle in his hand.

"Kyle?"

He glared at me. "What do you think you're doing?"

"What?"

"What do you think you're doing?"

My dance partner took a step back. "Yo, we were just dancing, dawg."

"Do I look like I'm ya dawg? Step the fuck off, nigga!"

I walked toward him. "Calm down! What are you doing?"

Others around us stopped dancing and began staring at us. The potential for this to go sideways and turn into a fight was real. My dance-off buddy shook his head and walked away, and then Kyle turned his glare toward me.

"Nah, what're you doing shaking ya ass all over that lame-ass nigga!"

I was shocked. "I wasn't shaking my ass on him, and don't talk to me like that!"

Kyle seemed even more irritated that I spoke up. "I'll talk to you any way I want! You just in here disrespecting me in front of all my frat brothers and shit!"

"You're drunk. No wonder you sound so stupid."

"Oh, I'm stupid now? C'mon, we're leaving!"

He grabbed my arm, and I pulled away. For the first time ever, I felt scared of him. He never touched me like that before.

"I'm not going anywhere with you acting like this! What's wrong with you?"

Brandon saw the commotion and darted toward us. "Hey, Kyle, what's going on?"

"Nothing, we were just leaving!"

"The hell we were!"

"Whoa, whoa, everybody, let's just calm down. Take a breath. Let's go outside and talk about this." Brandon pointed toward the door.

Kyle mean mugged him. "There isn't shit to talk about." He let out a long, deep breath. "Come on, she doesn't want to go with you. This isn't you, man. C'mon, man."

"This isn't none of your business, B!"

"You're both my friends. I don't want to see you both like this."

Brandon was trying his best to rationalize with him, trying to appeal to his better sense and the years of friendship they shared, but Kyle wasn't trying to hear that. He had a look of pure hatred in his eyes.

"What the fuck do you know about anything?"

"Really? Don't do this."

"Why not? Because you said so? That's my bitch!"

I cocked my head to the side. "Bitch? Fuck you!"

Brandon took a step back. "C'mon, man."

Kyle inched closer to him. "You supposed to be my boy, and you letting her disrespect me like that?"

"They were just dancing," he calmly replied.

I wasn't scared anymore. I was pissed. "You're making a total asshole out of yourself."

The bottle that was in his hand dropped to the floor and shattered. "Shut the fuck up!" Kyle gave me an evil glare, then lunged toward me.

Brandon instinctively blocked his path. "Yo! Chill!"

"Stop it!" I yelled, watching them lock arms, two Alpha males not backing down.

"Get the fuck off me!" Kyle pushed Brandon away.

"I'm not going to fight you, Kyle."

"I wouldn't want to fight me either, nigga! C'mon, Nia!"

"I'm not going anywhere with your drunk ass!"

Kyle once again lunged at me, but Brandon blocked his path again. That infuriated Kyle even more and he swung on Brandon, tagging his jaw. He staggered back and grabbed his face. I was blown.

"I told you to stay the fuck outta this!"

"Have it your way."

Brandon charged at Kyle and tackled him onto a table. They exchanged punches as they wreaked havoc in the living room. Folks with cell phones were already recording the fight, and I was expecting somebody to yell, "World Star," at any second. I watched in panic that one of them might get hurt. The crowd parted like the Red Sea as the two went at each other. In the midst of their scuffle, Kyle fell forward and hit his injured knee on the floor. The earth-shattering pain he must have felt caused him to yell out in a way I never heard before. Out of instinct I ran to him.

"Oh, my God, are you all right?"

"Get the fuck away from me!"

Kyle glared at me like I was the most disgusting thing he'd ever seen.

I looked at Brandon. "Are you okay?"

He wiped blood from his lips. "I'm fine."

"No, you're not." I walked toward him. "Come on."

I turned and looked at Kyle, who struggled to his feet.

"You know, B, I always knew you were a self-serving, backstabbing muthafucka!"

Brandon shook his head. I could tell that hurt him. All he was trying to do was stop his friend from making a mistake. I glared at Kyle with disgust and walked out.

"I can't believe that just happened."

"Well, my face does . . . ow."

"C'mon, let's get some ice on that."

It was about four thirty in the morning when I heard a knock on my door. I already knew who it was. I peeped out the hole and saw Kyle. I felt the hairs on the back of my neck stand up, and my heart started to race. For the second time tonight, I felt afraid of him. He looked a mess with his clothes still disheveled.

"What do you want?" I stood in the doorway with it cracked open.

"Baby, I'm sorry."

"Not good enough."

He whispered in a somber tone, "I know. I fucked up. Are you going to let me in?"

"No."

"Okay, I understand, but just hear me out."

"What are you going to tell me, Kyle? That it was the alcohol talking, not you? That you didn't mean to disrespect me in front of everybody? Or that punching your best friend was a mistake?"

"Baby, I was drunk and didn't mean those things I said."

"I think you did. Being drunk simply brought out everything you really wanted to say and do."

"Baby."

"You weren't just drunk. What the hell was that? I've never seen you act like that before."

"I just drank too much, and when I saw you with that other guy, I lost it. I don't know what came over me, but I swear on my momma, I will never do that to you again. You gotta believe me."

"I'm sorry, I don't. Every time you say you won't, you do."

"We can get past this. We can start over."

"I can't . . . I can't do this with you. You need help, Kyle, and I can't give it to you."

"What do you mean?"

He extended his arms to pull me close, but I pushed him away.

"You're up and down. You forget things. You think you tell me things when you didn't."

"That's not true."

"You seem angry and confused."

"I'm not."

"Something's not right." I looked at him and could tell he was getting aggravated. "How long were you playing football before college? How many bad hits have you had?"

"What difference does that make? I have a chance to go pro, and I have to take care of my family!"

"This is what I'm talking about. You're yelling for no reason."

He looked confused.

"Kyle, you're showing early signs of CTE. It's either that or you need to speak with a psychiatrist."

"What the fuck are you talking about? I don't need no fucking shrink!" He caught himself and backed down. "Don't do this, baby. We can get past this."

"Not right now we can't. Goodbye, Kyle."

I closed the door, locked it, and went back to my bedroom. I didn't even try to stop the tears from rolling down my face.

Chapter Thirteen

Shooting Pool

Nia Scott

Logging into my Facebook page, I saw that my inbox had about twenty unread messages. Half of them were WYD messages with dick pics attached. I didn't know why guys thought sending a woman their penis was going to make anyone want to get with them. *Deleted and blocked.* My DWS withstanding, I'd probably masturbated more this past month than most 15-year-old boys in Catholic school. Sadly, I'd actually gotten pretty good at it. I wasn't trying to hook up with these random weirdoes who had no idea how to hold a conversation with a woman.

It'd been about two and half months since Kyle and I broke up, and I was good. Sean was back home and told me everything was cool for now, but I could still hear the anger in his voice. Mom really pissed me off with the way that mess went down.

Sabina moved out. *Good riddance.* A part of me missed her company, but she was doing the most. I hoped she would slow down before things really went sideways.

Brandon and I still talked on a regular basis. I found out from him that Kyle didn't get the job in Gainesville. A few of the messages in my inbox were from him, but I'd been too afraid to open them. As a result, he'd been sending flowers, candy, stuffed animals, and every other cute thing he could think of. All of which ended up in my garbage. Well, except for the candy. I ate the candy. No sense in that going to waste. As much as I missed him, I knew he hadn't changed. With each day that went by, I thought about him less. I made the right decision.

I went to my room, grabbed a towel, took off my clothes, walked to the bathroom, and turned on the shower. With my cell in my hand, I sat on the toilet and continued to scroll my timeline. Brandon and I were going to hang out tonight. I really hadn't gone out since the frat party. I needed to focus more on school anyway. Truth was I was in a bit of a funk. I wondered if he ever thought about what almost happened between us. I had a lot more recently than I wanted to admit. Now I was starting to wonder how things would be if we did.

I finally got in the shower and let the streams of water wash over me. Why did this showerhead feel so good all of a sudden? A portable, adjustable, vibrating showerhead. I got it because it was a good deal and for nothing else. *Lord, I wonder what this setting does.* I flipped to another setting, and it became alive in my hand. *Has my sex life really come to this?* I laughed. Wow, as if I needed any excuse to masturbate more.

After I was done, I wrapped myself in the plush towel and painted my toenails a nice shade of burgundy. As I was finishing, the doorbell rang, and I walked on my heels to the door.

"Hey, what's up, homie?"

Brandon was kinda thrown off guard by seeing me in nothing but a towel. His mouth hung open, and I grinned at his reaction.

"Hey, come in. I'm almost done with my toes."

I turned and shuffled back to the couch. He walked in and sat on the La-Z-Boy across from me. I enjoyed watching his struggle to keep his gaze on my face.

"So where are we going again?"

"Ah, bowling. We're going bowling."

"Great, so I'm going to have to put on them ugly shoes. I don't even know why I bothered to do my toes." I glanced at his sneakers. "The Thirteen Retro Playoffs? Nice."

Brandon looked at me, somewhat shocked. "Thanks. I didn't know you were a sneaker head."

"I wouldn't say that, but I do got a bit of a fetish for them. Plus my little brother got every damn pair of Jordans."

I rested my foot on the coffee table in front of me, showing a bit more leg, and Brandon's eyes got wide like saucers. I was having way too much fun. "Did you finish your paper for Professor Miller?"

"Yeah." He cleared his throat. "Last night. What about you?"

"Yes, sir. I've had a lot of free time on my hands."

"Too much."

"What's that supposed to mean?"

"It means you been hiding in here too long."

I leaned forward. "I'm not hiding."

His eyes scanned my body once again, and he adjusted himself in the chair. "Yeah, okay. So, ah, I thought you said you'll be ready when I got here."

"Oh, I lost track of time in the shower. It'll take me a minute to get dressed."

I got up and walked to my bedroom. After a few minutes I emerged wearing fitted blue jeans with a white tank top, and a smile spread across his face.

"I'm ready."

"Yes, you are."

Brandon took me to Ten Pen in Atlantic Station. I loved coming down here to shop at H&M and Old Navy. When we walked inside, we were shocked at how crowded it was. Every lane was taken.

I said joyfully, "Ah, too bad, no smelly shoes."

"You want to shoot some pool?"

"Sure. I'm a little rusty though."

He chuckled. "You can't be that bad."

"No, you don't understand. When I say rusty, I mean I suck," I clarified for him.

"Oh, so we got to do it now." Brandon took my hand and led me toward the pool room. He placed the balls in the plastic triangle holder and set them up on the table. I couldn't believe how much I was about to humiliate myself in front of him, but I didn't mind. If I was going to make a fool of myself, I was going to do it with confidence.

He looked at me. "Okay, you ready to break?"

"Huh? You talking to me?"

"No, the other chick I came with. Yeah, you! C'mon."

"Okay," I sighed. "I warned you."

I picked up the cue stick and gripped it like a weapon.

"Ah, Nia, you might wanna hold it—"

"Shhh! Don't bother me. I'm trying to shoot here."

He shook his head. "All right."

I shot and missed the ball. "Oops! It's all right. I got it."

I tapped the ball, and it rolled to the left. I glanced at his face, and he was trying to hold back a laugh. *Whatever!*

"Ah, I think this table is slanted," I told him seriously.

"Yeah, right. Slanted."

Brandon took a shot, and two balls went into a hole. He glanced at me and grinned. "Must be the table."

"Funny," I dryly replied.

"So how have you been feeling?" Brandon took another shot, and another ball disappeared into a hole.

"You know, since this summer I've had nothing but drama in my life, but now I feel stress free."

"I saw Kyle the other day."

"Did he say anything to you?"

"Nah. Just glared at me, gave me the middle finger, and walked away. I don't think he's fucking with me anymore."

"You think not?"

We both laughed, and he finally missed a shot. "Sometimes you gotta let some people go for your own good."

I picked up my cue stick. "I got it this time." I shot again and hit the ball, but it barely moved. *I suck so bad it's not even funny.* "Oh, c'mon!"

"Okay, okay, let me show you." Brandon moved behind me and placed his arms around my waist. Then he took my hands and placed them correctly on the cue stick. The scent of his cologne filled my nostrils, and I liked it. Feeling him next to me again felt nice. Last time we were this close, we were half naked.

"All right, take your time and aim the ball where you want it to go. It's all about angles. Learning to play pool is like learning trig."

"What?"

"Yeah, this is stroke mechanics. It's angle, speed, and spin. Kinda like sex in a way if you think about it."

I chuckled. "Oh, so this is what you guys do? Trying to find that right angle to sink that thang in a hole?"

His mouth was by my ear. "Yeah, but if you know how to stroke it right, it goes in every time."

I stroked the cue stick and hit the ball in the pocket. "Yes!"

"See what I told you?"

"Thanks."

I stared at him over my shoulder. Brandon forgot that he was still holding me, even though I didn't mind. Then he realized and let me go. "No problem."

I smiled and shot again. Oh God, it felt so good, him holding me. I was aroused. *Fuck that damn showerhead.*

This is the real thing. I haven't felt this turned on in a while.

We continued to play, and of course he won. I didn't care because sex was on my mind, and I knew it was on his. I was weighing my options. If we had sex, it would change everything about our friendship. Would I look like a ho hooking up with my ex-boyfriend's former best friend? Yep. I would be called everything but a child of God on Black Twitter, but did I care? Not really.

After about three hours at Atlantic Station, Brandon took me home. I had fun, something I hadn't had in a while. I was glad I let him talk me into going out. As I reached my door, I glanced at him. I didn't want this night to end.

"You were getting kinda good there."

I was genuinely happy to hear him say that. "You think so? Maybe we should play more often."

"Well, I can stop holding back."

"Whatever. I'm eventually going to get good and whoop yo' ass." I opened the door.

"I bet you will. Good times."

We gazed at each other intensely.

"This is strange, huh?"

He nodded. "Yeah, we're both grown and single, so this shouldn't be awkward, right?"

"I know, but if I invite you in, everything changes."

"Is that a bad thing?" he asked.

"No." There was an awkward silence between us. "We've both been feeling this for a while, and now I can't think of a reason why we shouldn't see where it goes."

"There's not a reason in the world."

He leaned in and kissed my lips, and I felt so turned on. *My DWS is about to be cured.*

The next thing I knew, Brandon and I were walking into the apartment toward my bedroom. This time

I kissed him. Kissed him like I wanted him more than a slice of Hershey cheesecake. His hands reached around me and unbuttoned my jeans. I stepped back, pulled them down, and took off my top. I didn't have a bra on. He gazed at my breasts and grinned. He unbuttoned his shirt and pulled it off. I stared at his chest and smiled. He walked toward me and put his lips on my neck and breasts, then found my erect nipples. I found his belt buckle and unfastened it. Searching for that magic cue stick of his, I found it, and my oh my. I stepped back and looked at his erection in my hand and smiled like a kid on Christmas morning.

"You like?"

I bit my bottom lip. "Yeah, I likey." I went to my dresser and got a condom.

He beamed. "I've got one of those already."

"Good. You're going to need more than one tonight."

I touched his hardness. He hissed as I rubbed his ridged flesh. I felt myself getting moist with anticipation of what he was going to feel like inside me. He took the condom I gave him, opened it, and rolled it on. We kissed and caressed each other until we made it to my bed. We crawled on top of the mattress. His body on top of mine felt so right. I parted my thighs and felt him pushing inside me. I moaned. He groaned. More of his erection sank inside of me.

I whispered, "Remember, it's all about angle, speed, and spin."

He looked at me with lustful eyes. "Oh, you mean like this?"

I sang a heavenly tune as I felt him stroke deep inside of me. And finally, after so long, Brandon and I were making love under my sheets. Most guys exaggerate about their bedroom skills, but Brandon was all action. Obviously, he had put a lot of thought into what he would do to me if we ever hooked up as he positioned me from side to side. Shit, I had a wish list too, and we took turns fulfilling those wishes. I didn't know if it was the excitement of being with someone new or if it was because we wanted each other for so long, but our sex was amazing. I was dealing with my own orgasm when Brandon grunted loudly as he climaxed, then collapsed on top of me. We rested in each other's arms until he caught his second wind, then put the second condom to use.

Later that night, we were lying in my bed, spent.

"You good?"

"I am now." I had a big ol' grin on my face.

We were quiet for a while, just being in the moment.

"I didn't want to bring it up before, but are we going to talk about the elephant in the room?" he asked.

"Kyle? Yeah, I guess we should. Do you feel some type of way about it?"

"You mean guilty? Sorta. He is . . . well, he was my friend."

"And he was my boyfriend. He's made it quite clear you're no longer his friend, and I'm not going back to him, so what do we do?"

He pulled me closer. "We do us. Let's try not to put it in his face."

"Are we creeping?"

"Nah, we're keeping this to ourselves for now."

I sighed. "You know people are going to have plenty to say later on."

"Let them. We aren't living our lives for anybody else."

Chapter Fourteen

The Social Media Warrior

Nia Scott

I awoke with a slight cramp. For the past week this bitch Aunt Flo had been messing with me. As usual, her timing was freaking perfect. I was craving to be with Brandon again. We'd been hanging out together since that night, not having sex, and it was driving me crazy.

I went in the bathroom, checked my pad, and it looked like Auntie was on her way out. A smile came across my face as I jumped in the shower. Afterward, I checked my phone and saw that I was tagged by one of my Facebook friends, Dedra, in a post. She was actually somebody I knew in real life and was a student here at Clark. She considered herself "woke," a term I really didn't like. Being "woke" is more or less the act of being very pretentious about how much you care about a social issue.

I considered myself "aware" of the issues we face. Dedra was very pro-Black on social media. Most of her posts were pointing out racism and Black folks in the media she thought were cooning. Funny thing was, I agreed with a lot of her viewpoints, but she was very judgmental and left no room for redemption in her stance. I clicked on the video and watched it. The video was of a White woman in Walmart caught on camera harassing a group of Black students. The woman, who the internet named "Walmart Wanda," was recorded telling the Black shoppers that they "don't belong here" and accusing them of shoplifting. The footage on Facebook was reposted and shared on Twitter, Instagram, and YouTube as the latest in a long series of videos posted to social media showing White women like "BBQ Becky," "Permit Patty," "Corner Store Caroline" not minding their own business and confronting Black people for no reason.

I was disgusted by it all. After I fixed a quick breakfast, I was out the door, heading to class. I was dying to see Brandon to let him know that Auntie was gone and I needed some!

As I was walking through the quad, I saw Brandon, and then I saw who he was talking to—Dedra. She was showing him something on her phone and touching his arm. I could tell by the way she was gazing at him that she was feeling him. I suddenly felt something I never felt when it came to him: jealousy. I didn't like the way she was touching my man. Not that I thought Brandon was cheating on me with her, but she was an attractive woman: a curvy, chocolate sista who was thick. Every time I saw her, she would be going on and on about some dude she wanted to fuck at her gym who obviously didn't want to fuck her. Probably because she was annoying as hell to be around. At any rate, she was now playing with my bone, and I was not into sharing.

I strolled toward them. "What's up, y'all?"

Brandon lit up seeing me. "Hey."

Dedra glanced at me. "Hey, Nia, did you see the post I tagged you in?"

"Yeah, I watched it this morning. What's wrong with these people?"

"Nothing but racist-ass White folks. Can't stand to see Black people winning."

"Dedra was just showing me the video," Brandon offered. "I'm not even shocked anymore."

I nodded. "I know, right."

Dedra gave me a smug look. "So you and Kyle haven't gotten back together yet?"

I glared at her. I couldn't believe she asked me that like it was any of her business. "Nah, we're not together."

"It's a shame brothers like that rarely stay with their own kind. He's probably with a White girl. You know what they say, 'All skin folk ain't kinfolk.'"

A small part of me wanted to tell her to shut the fuck up, but then I remembered I didn't care what she thought. "I don't know who Kyle is with and don't care."

"I'm just saying I was surprised he wasn't with a light or damn near White girl instead of a brown-skinned girl like you."

"A brown-skinned girl like me?"

"Yeah." She stepped back with a shit-eating smirk on her face and looked me up and down. "You know what I mean. A sista with melanin. You know how they do. When they're on top, light or White is always right. But when they're hurt, they always go back to their roots. Don't worry, girl. I'm sure a fine girl like you will snag another NFL prospect soon."

I folded my arms. "What makes you think I'm looking for a football player?"

"I thought that was your type. It's okay. We all have one."

"Oh." I grinned. "So what's your type?"

"Well," she said, smirking, "I like intellectual chocolate brothers. The kind of guys who can handle all this melanin." She turned her gaze back toward Brandon. "So I wanted to know if you're coming to the party tonight at the Basement?"

"I don't know." He glanced at me. "What do you wanna do, babe?" He put his arms around me.

"Whatever you want to do."

Dedra's mouth fell open. "Oh, so you two are together?"

I gave her a cocky smirk. "Yep."

She looked us up and down. "Wow, so you got with the best friend, huh? That's interesting."

"I know, right? He's not an NFL prospect, but I snagged him anyway. Anything else you want to know or have to say?" I crossed my arms, waiting for an answer. She rolled her eyes but said nothing.

"About that party," Brandon interjected, seeing my body language, "I might be busy. I'll talk to you later."

"Yeah, whatever," she mumbled and strolled off, making sure Brandon saw every twist and turn of her ass. Our eyes met each other's, and we both suppressed a laugh.

"What happened to us keeping it on the low?"

"I have to let these lonely chicks know I got a lady. Besides, she's really irritating."

I laughed. "Good, because I really didn't like the way she was all up on you anyway. Thirsty bitch."

We turned and started walking. "Anyway, how are you?"

"I'm good. My Aunt Flo packed her bags this morning."

He licked his lips and pulled me close. "Oh, really? So how about we skip going to the Basement and let me slide inside your basement tonight?"

"Now that's a party."

Chapter Fifteen

Forgive Me

Nia Scott

I awoke in his arms after another night of making love. For the last month this had become our routine, and I loved it. Brandon was practically living with me, and for some reason I didn't mind. It was strange that I never felt comfortable with the idea of Kyle and me living together, but somehow this felt right. I stared at his handsome face and smiled. His eyes fluttered as he focused on me.

He smiled. "Morning."

"Hey."

"You're up early." He stroked my hair.

"I seem to have a lot of energy these days."

"Yeah, I've noticed."

"I appreciate it."

"You've been appreciating the hell outta me, and I love it."

We laughed, and he sat up in bed.

"You hungry?"

"Yeah, I can eat."

He came in for a kiss, and I covered my mouth.

"I got morning breath!"

He rolled his eyes. "I don't care!"

I tried to roll away from him, and he grabbed me and pulled me closer. We started laughing and wrestling as he finally pinned me down and kissed me.

"My breath is funky!"

"So what? So is mine. We got morning breath, but guess what else I got?"

"What?"

He smiled. "Morning wood."

"Oh, well, let's see where we can put that to the most good."

My hand found his wonderful erection, and we began to explore each other's anatomy again.

A week later, I was in Cumberland Mall doing a little shopping in Sephora. After I was done, I was walking out through the food court area when I saw him. Our eyes met, and I instantly felt uneasy. I couldn't just turn around and walk the other way. That would be even more awkward. Kyle started walking toward me, and I exhaled.

"Hey."

"Hi."

"How you been?"

"Fine, and you?"

"I've been better. Been missing you." Kyle reached to caress my face, but I pulled away.

"Kyle, don't do that."

"Do what? Show you affection? I can't stop feeling what I do for you. I know I messed things up between us, but I still love you."

"I'm sorry you feel that way, but I've moved on. You should too."

He frowned. "With who?"

"It doesn't matter. What we had was special, but it was too much."

He glared at me. "Then say you don't love me and you never have. Just say it. That's all you have to say."

Here it was, the moment I knew would eventually come. I couldn't lie to him. I couldn't do that to him. He deserved to know the truth and to hear it from me.

"I'll always love you, but I'm not in love with you. I'm with somebody who cares for me a lot, and I care about him too."

He stared at me in silence, and I continued.

"We didn't plan for it to happen, but it did."

"You trifling bitch. You're fucking Brandon. My best friend! Who does that?"

"Your best friend? The one you tried to beat to death?" I looked at him seriously.

"You know what?" He pointed a finger in my face. "Fuck you and fuck him." He stormed off angrily.

No matter how he may feel about me, he hasn't changed at all. I'm so glad I'm out of that relationship. There was too much drama between us. When I thought about it, I hadn't been happy with Kyle in a long time, but now I questioned if I was ever happy. Finding out about Brii was a major change in our dynamics, but then maybe it was for the best.

Later that night I decided to check up on my brother. I hadn't really spoken to my mother since the big blowup a few months ago. Brandon was in the kitchen cooking while I was on the sofa with my cell to my ear.

"I'll be home for Christmas break."

"It'll be good to see you, sis."

"So how's Dad? I haven't called him in a while."

"He's good, and we worked things out, so I stay with him on the weekends."

"That's good." I paused for a moment. "Sean, is Dad still dating Brandi?"

"The one with the pretty face and big titties?"

I rolled my eyes. "Yeah, her."

"Actually, I don't think so. It's been a minute since I've seen him with her."

"Oh, wow." That was interesting to hear. My dad had been dating Brandi for a while. He told me she was a paralegal he met through a mutual friend. I met her over the summer. From what I could tell, they seemed to click with each other. Unlike Leon, she was really cool. *I wonder what happened. I'll have to ask him about it the next time we speak.* "Anyway, how's your game been?"

"It couldn't be better," he said confidently. "I'm still pulling my triple doubles every night."

"And what about things with Leon?"

"Cool for now. I think he's glad I'm not here as much, but when I am, we don't say shit to each other."

"And Mom is still acting like everything's fine?"

"Do you even have to ask?"

I sighed and shook my head in disbelief.

Brandon walked toward me with a spoon of chili and fed it to me. Damn, it tasted so good. If I had known he was this good in the kitchen, I would've had him cooking for me.

I turned my attention back to my call. "Just continue to focus on school and basketball."

"That's all I can do. Well, sis, I gotta get going."

"Okay, I'll talk to you later. Love you."

"Love you too."

I ended the call and looked at Brandon, who had a grin on his face.

"So I'm going to meet the parents?"

I sighed. "Only if you want to."

"That'll be cool with me. How's your brother?"

"He's good for now."

He took my hand, pulled me to my feet, and walked me to the table. "Hey, have a seat. You're about to eat my dorm-famous chili."

"Dorm-famous? Why am I just learning about this?"

"Can't let all my culinary arts skills out of the bag at once."

"Go ahead, Mr. Chef Boyardee."

"What did I tell you about doubting my skills?"

"Just because you're good in the bedroom didn't mean it carried over to the kitchen."

"Good, huh?" He dished out a bowl of chili for me, then himself, then grabbed a bag of tortilla scoops. "You still got that limp when you walk, don't you?"

I smiled, and he sat with me at the table, and we began to eat. It was delicious. I glanced at him. "Do you ever have second thoughts about your major?"

He nodded. "I'll be lying if I said no. Are you having doubts?"

"I don't know. I mean, sometimes. I wonder what my reasons were for going into medicine. This was a love of mine since I was nine years old. Now I question whether I still feel the same."

"Well, do you?"

"Most of the time I do." I sighed. "Then there are days when I feel all this pressure, and I get frustrated."

"How do you think you can change that?"

I shrugged my shoulders. "I don't know. I'm still trying to figure it out."

"Well, just know I'm here for you."

I looked at Brandon and smiled. "I know. It feels so different to be in a relationship that's not one-sided. I was constantly worrying about Kyle, and he never tried to understand what I was going through. It's nice to be with someone who truly cares about how I feel. That makes me happy." I kissed him, and he picked me up and walked toward the bedroom.

"What about the chili?"

He glanced back at the table. "Aahhh, it's not that great anyway."

It was a few weeks before Christmas, and I was taking an Uber from a boutique in Decatur to my apartment. My cell phone rang. I looked at it and saw Kyle's number. I pushed ignore. Immediately, he called back. *Why is he calling me?* I stared at it for a second and then reluctantly answered it.

"Hello?"

No answer.

"Kyle, is this you?"

"Nia . . ." His voice was low and kind of slurred.

"Why do you sound like that?"

"I just . . . want to say I'm sorry . . . for everything I did to you . . . to us."

The driver changed lanes. "Sorry for what? Kyle, what are you talking about? Are you all right?"

In a slurred voice, he replied, "I'm sorry . . . I loved you. You deserved better than me. I'm a fuckup. I know that now. I fuck up everything I touch."

I rolled my eyes. *Here he is playing victim again,* I said to myself. "Did you take some of your Vicodin?"

"Yeah."

"How much did you take?"

His voice was very low. "Goodbye, Nia."

The call ended. I redialed his number, but he didn't answer. I rode for a moment in silence, thinking about his words. That goodbye didn't sit well with my soul. There was a finality about it I didn't like, so I called Brandon.

"What's up, baby?"

"Hey, I just got a weird call from Kyle. He didn't sound too good."

"What did he say?"

"He was apologizing for everything, but his words were all slurred. I think he took something."

He exhaled. "That's just great. Where are you now?"

"I'm in an Uber. I was heading back to my place, but can you meet me at his?"

"Yeah, I can be there in ten minutes. Should we call nine-one-one?" he asked.

"I think you should. He sounded bad."

"All right, I'm on my way."

I ended the call and told the Uber driver to make a detour and gave him Kyle's address. *What the hell has he done now? I hope he hasn't done something stupid.*

When I arrived at his apartment building, I sprinted to his door. I knocked, but there was no answer. Again I knocked. I waited a moment with no reply. Now I was nervous. What if he tried to overdose on his medicine?

"Kyle, open up! Come on."

On a whim, I tried the doorknob, and to my surprise, it turned completely. I walked in, and his apartment was dark. All the blinds were closed. I flicked on the lights and walked farther inside. His place was a mess. His clothes were all over. He was normally a neat freak.

"Kyle?"

I opened his bedroom door and saw him sitting in semi darkness. I took a step closer. The blinds on the window were half open, and I spotted an empty bottle on the floor. I paused when I saw a gun in his hand. My heart started thumping rapidly in my chest.

"You shouldn't be here, Nia."

"Kyle, what are you doing?"

"I'm doing what I should have done a long time ago."

"We can talk about this . . . about anything. I'm here."

"You're so beautiful. Did I ever really tell you that before?"

"Yeah, plenty of times. Listen to me, just put the gun down and come with me."

He tightened his grip on it. "I should've treated you better. You deserved so much more than . . . I could ever give you."

"You don't have to give me anything. Just put the gun down."

My cell started to ring.

"You'd better answer that. Might be B."

I looked at my phone and nervously answered it. "Hey."

"I'm almost there. What's going on?"

"He has a gun."

"What! Get the hell outta there now!" Brandon yelled into the phone.

I stared into Kyle's eyes. "I'm all right. We're all right."

"No, you're not! Get outta there!"

"Just get here." I ended the call.

Kyle smirked. "You know I was mad about you two . . . at first . . . but I know he's better for you than I am. He can give you what you need."

"You don't have to do this because of us." I took a few steps closer to him.

"I don't have anything left. I can't play football. I can't go back home and face everybody . . . and I don't have you."

"What are you talking about? You have everything. You always told me it's not about how hard you get knocked down. It's all about getting back up. And you have! You're not thinking straight right now because of the drugs."

He smiled. "I wrote a letter to my mom. You'll make sure she gets it, won't you?"

"No. You'll tell her yourself. Kyle, if you love me, you won't do this to yourself or me."

"This is the best for both of us."

I heard the front door open. "Nia!" Brandon yelled.

"Forgive me," Kyle said softly.

"Kyle, don't do this. Please don't—" I begged.

As Kyle raised the gun to his temple, everything seemed to move in slow motion. I tried to move toward him. Brandon rushed into the bedroom behind me. My eyes widened as the air rushed from my lungs in a desperate scream I knew would come too late. The sound of the gun cutting through the air was deafening. My eyes witnessed the unbelievable. Kyle's body fell off the edge of the bed and went limp on the floor.

I heard Brandon behind me. "Oh, my God!"

My ears rang, and tears filled my eyes as I grabbed a sheet off the bed and held it to his head to stop the bleeding. I was crying and screaming hysterically.

"Nia!"

I glanced at him. "I . . . I gotta try to stop the bleeding! Help me."

Brandon didn't move. It didn't register to me, but he had already realized that the worst was over. He saw the brain matter on the floor. I did too, but I wouldn't accept that Kyle was gone. I heard sirens getting louder as I tried to stop his bleeding. My hands were soaked in his blood.

"Nia, you can stop."

"What the fuck are you talking about? Help me!"

Brandon knelt down behind me and touched my back.

"What are you doing? We have to help him!"

"He's gone."

"No, no!"

Brandon wrapped his arms around me as I broke down. Was this happening for real? Why me? Why him? *What have I done?*

Chapter Sixteen

So Many Tears

Brandon Griffin

It'd been a week since Kyle's death, and Nia hadn't said two words. I took some time off school and wished I had somebody to talk to about this shit. I lost my best friend, even though he hated me. I couldn't blame him. I couldn't help, and I wished that Kyle were still alive. For all his ill ways, he was still my friend. I remembered when Kyle tried to hook me up with Sabina when I first met her. After we went out, it was obvious to both of us we weren't right for each other, but Kyle wasn't trying to hear it. I recalled that conversation like it was yesterday.

"Did you hit that ass?" asked Kyle with a shit-eating grin on his face.

I laughed. "Nah, I wasn't really feeling her like that."

He stared at me as if I were crazy. "What! You're not feeling her? Did you feel that ass she got?"

"Of course, but she's not my type."

"Not your type? My dude, all that ass she got makes her everybody's type. You ain't trying to find the future Mrs. Griffin! You coulda fucked. I know you could've. I saw the way she was pushing up on you at the apartment."

"Yeah, I could've but . . . I don't know, man. I wasn't in the mood to go through all that."

"Man, you slipping! If I were you, I woulda had Sabina ass up, face down. And she Indian, too? You know how freaky they be with that Kama Sutra shit."

"Really, bruh?" I laughed. "She's not the one."

He scoffed. "I know what it is. You got your eye on some new booty, don't ya?"

I chuckled.

"Yeaaah, I know you, dog! Who is she?"

"Man, I'm not checking for no other girl now."

He smirked. "Whatever. I know you better than you think I do."

I shook my head, trying to erase the memory. An overwhelming feeling of guilt consumed me. Kyle was right. I did have my eye on somebody else. But I couldn't tell him it was Nia. I really had it in my mind to get with Sabina that night, but I couldn't do it. Nia was the only thing I could think about at that point. When we ended up in my dorm room after they fought, I knew I had made the right decision about not getting with Sabina. It wasn't like I planned to take Nia away from Kyle, but I knew he was going to lose her. He was his own worst enemy, and maybe I was a backstabber. Who knew?

The night we fought hurt me more than Nia knew. Ending that friendship hurt. I never told Nia that I blamed myself for Kyle's suicide, too. I took his girl, his whole world away from him. Some of our mutual friends told me when they split up that he was taking antidepressants. I never said anything to Nia because I didn't want to risk losing her. I was afraid she would go back to him. Maybe that was selfish, but I wasn't going to risk losing her. In a way, his suicide was on me. I saw the path he was on and could've tried harder to save him, but I didn't. I never told Nia I cried like a baby alone in my room the night Kyle died.

Our relationship had grown so much over the last few months. *How do we deal with this?* No matter how many times I told Nia this was not her fault, she would still blame herself. That was just how she was. She thought that she could have done something to prevent this from happening. It was going to be hard for her to get over seeing Kyle take his own life. *Shit, I'm not sure I will ever get over that.*

I was going to get some counseling so I could start to process it all, but I didn't think Nia was going to do that. She was heading back to Chicago for the holidays, and from the way she had been, I wasn't sure if she was going to come back.

Chapter Seventeen

Home Again

Nia Scott

Chicago

The doctors said that Kyle was abusing his Vicodin and taking antidepressants, which I never knew about. I should've. With his erratic behavior, mood swings, and forgetfulness, I often wondered if I was right about him developing CTE. It was impossible to determine that with the brain damage from the gunshot wound. After his funeral in Atlanta, I took some time off from school and went back to Chicago. I didn't know what to say to his mother. What the hell could I say to her? I just stood there and watched her cry.

Brandon called me every other day to check up on me and let me know he would give me time to deal with everything. In hindsight now, we shouldn't have gotten together. We probably pushed Kyle over the edge.

According to my mother, Leon had been out of work for four months now and claimed he was looking for a new job every day. Judging by the hours he spent in front of the TV watching *Judge Judy*, it didn't look like he was making much of an effort to find one either. Meanwhile, my mother was working overtime to take care of this jackass.

Since I'd been home, I'd been my mother's Uber driver. After running a few errands, I pulled into our driveway and went inside. There he was, perched on the couch doing jury duty for *Judge Judy* again. He hadn't said much of anything to me, but I saw in his face that he couldn't stand I was back home. He glanced at me as I headed to the kitchen. I grabbed a bottled water and a bag of chips, then walked back into the living room.

"Hey, do you know why your mother didn't pay the electric bill yet?" He waved what looked like an overdue notice at me.

I glared at his dusty ass. "Do you know why you haven't found a job yet?"

He didn't respond but scowled at me. *Fuck you too. Get up off your ass and get a job.* I went upstairs to get away from him before something unpleasant came from my mouth.

I spoke to a counselor after Kyle's death and learned that it was normal after witnessing a suicide to be vulnerable to depression and self-harm. I wasn't going to harm myself, but I was depressed. I lay spread-eagle on my bed, then heard a knock at the door.

"Who is it?"

"Yo, it's me!" Sean's voice resonated through the door.

"Come in." I really didn't want to talk to anybody, but I pulled myself together.

"Kind of early to be going to bed, isn't it?"

"I'm not. I'm just lying down. What's up?"

He came and sat next to me. "Nothing, I just wanted to see how you're doing."

I smiled. "I'm fine, Sean. You really don't have to check up on me."

"Well, you know, if you want to talk about anything, I'm here."

I could tell he wanted to be there for me the way I was for him, but I couldn't tell him how I felt inside when I didn't really know myself.

"There's not much to say. Listen, baby brother, please don't worry about me. I will be okay. You just focus on school and your post-up game. It can use some work."

He laughed. "Whatever! You always have my back, so I want you to know I got yours."

"Thanks." I kissed his cheek.

We heard our mother coming through the front door. She must have taken an Uber home. She knocked on my bedroom door and opened it slightly. "Hey, guys."

"Hey, Mom," I responded.

"I gotta finish some homework." Sean got up and walked out without saying anything to her.

She sighed and sat on the bed next to me. "He hates me, doesn't he?"

"No, he doesn't."

"Then why is he so angry at me?"

I folded my arms. "You know why, Mom."

She sighed. "He has to learn to accept him now."

"I really don't want to talk about it." I rolled my eyes and turned my back toward her.

"Will somebody please talk to me? I am the mother here."

I turned over and looked at her. "Nobody is talking to you because nothing ever changes."

"All right." She sighed again. "How are you doing?"

"Are you and Sean taking turns at this?"

"Taking turns at what?"

"He just asked me the same question. I'm fine."

"Are you sure? Because all you do is stay up in this room. You're barely eating anything."

"My ex-boyfriend blew his brains out in front of me, so I might need a minute," I told her sarcastically.

"You can't blame yourself for that. Kyle made a bad choice."

"You have no idea how I'm feeling, and you barely knew him! You met him, what, one or two times at the most? You didn't know him, Mom. You only saw what you wanted, and that was for me to marry him because of football. You don't know what I went through, so please stop trying to be Iyanla Vanzant!"

As soon as the words left my mouth, I regretted them. She didn't deserve that, but I couldn't help myself. There was an awkward silence, and my mother got up off my bed.

"I'll have dinner ready soon." She turned and walked out.

Damn, I'm such a bitch. It's like I can't filter my mouth with her.

About an hour later, I smelled fried chicken in the air, and my stomach growled. I went downstairs and saw Mom making a plate for Leon as I had a seat at the dining room table.

She smiled seeing me. "Are you hungry?"

"Yeah, I'll have a little."

Leon stared at his plate and sighed. "Did you make some rice without the peas?"

"Oh, I forgot to make a separate pot of white rice."

"You know I don't like the peas."

She shook her head. "I'm sorry. I'm doing a thousand things at once."

"So you're not going to make some more rice?"

I rolled my eyes. "Why don't you just pick the peas out?"

He glanced at me with annoyance, then glanced back at her.

Mom picked up his plate. "Don't worry about it. I'll make some more. It'll be a few more minutes."

Sean came downstairs with his basketball under his arm. "Hey, Mom, I'm going to go by Bryan's house for a minute, okay?"

"You're not going to eat first?"

"Nah, I'm not hungry. I'll eat when I get back."

"Sit down and eat your food," Leon commanded sternly.

"I'm not hungry, man."

With more bass in his tone, he continued, "Your mother cooked all this food. Now sit down and eat."

Ignoring him, he looked at Mom. "Mom, I'll eat when I get back in. Promise."

"I'm talking to you. Sit down and eat!" Leon rose out of his chair like he was going to do something, and I did too.

"He said he isn't hungry, so leave him alone."

His head craned toward me. "Stay out of this, Nia. Sit down!"

My face scowled. "Stay out of it? Who do you think you're talking to? That's my brother, and you're not his father!"

My mother rushed toward Leon. "All right, everybody, just settle down."

"You're just going to let him talk to us like that?"

She exhaled. "Nia, please."

Leon glared at me. "If you don't like the way I talk, that's too bad, but he's going to sit down and eat with this family."

"Nigga, you ain't no part of this family. You just some house guest!"

Leon pointed his finger at Sean. "If you walk out, don't come back!"

"You sorry son of a bitch! You sit on your ass all day, then got the nerve to try to kick my brother out? Go to hell!"

Sean chuckled. "Yo, I'm out."

"Sean!"

He marched out the door. Leon walked out of the dining room, and I stared at my mom.

"This is exactly why Sean doesn't want to be here."

"If he would just try to listen—"

"What! Listen to him? Are you kidding me? I wish you had Sean's back like you have his. He's kicking your son out of your house, and you're not doing anything about it!"

"Leon is not kicking him out. Everybody needs to calm down."

"No, you just need to open your eyes."

Every time I thought I was being unfair to my mother, she went and did something like this, and I felt like, *nope, I'm right.* She acted like she had no backbone at all.

I found Sean at his friend's house pissed off, so I brought him home later that night. I wished Leon had said something to him or me. I'd have kicked his lame ass out myself!

Chapter Eighteen

Family Feud

Nia Scott

Since I decided to take the semester off from school, I needed to get a job. Even though my father paid for my breaking my apartment lease and he said he was still going to put money in my account, I wanted to work, so I got a little job at Macy's. Between putting clothes on the rack and dressing the mannequins in the ladies' section, time flew by. After that, I headed to the food court in the mall and got some teriyaki chicken. My cell started to vibrate, and I saw his face on the caller ID.

"Hey, Brandon."

"Hey, you're hard to catch up with these days."

"I'm at work. On break now."

"I've missed you."

I exhaled. "I've missed you too."

"Have you decided when you're going to come back?"

"I . . . I'm thinking about maybe this fall."

"Fall? I didn't think you would be gone for so long."

"I know. I just want to spend some more time with my brother. He's been going through a lot with Mom and Leon. I'm all he has, ya know?"

"Yeah, I understand, but what about you? You have one semester left. Then wasn't it Emory University in the fall?"

"Yeah, that's still the plan. I'm just pushing it back a little."

He sighed. "I'm not trying to rush you. I just don't want you to lose focus on what you want, and I don't wanna lose you either."

"I don't want you to feel like, you know, you have to be loyal to me or some shit. I mean, if you meet another girl—"

"There isn't anybody else, and I'm not looking to meet anybody else."

Tears started to fill my eyes. "Okay, well, I . . . gotta go. My break is over."

"All right. I love you. I'll call you later."

"Okay, bye."

I ended the call and wiped my eyes. *Damn, why did he have to say that? I want to be with him so much, but it's not right.* Kyle killed himself because I was too selfish to see past my own desires. I couldn't do that again. Being with Brandon was a mistake. I might as well have pulled the trigger myself.

With my part-time hours at Macy's, it still made sense for me to drop my mother off and pick her up from work. I was still not happy with her, and she knew it. We were barely speaking to each other at this point. This shit with Leon drove a huge wedge in our family. Why couldn't she see that? Did she even want to? With all the shade I was throwing her, I was surprised she was trying to start up a conversation with me on the drive home.

"How was your day, Nia?"

"Fine."

"Did you have a bad day?"

"Nope."

"Have you spoken to Brandon lately?"

"He actually called me today."

She looked at me curiously. "Everything okay?"

"Yeah."

"Do you still care about him?"

"Yes."

"Do you miss him?"

"Yes."

She caught herself before she said anything else. Usually this would have been a perfect time for my mother to tell me I shouldn't let him go, but now she wanted to bite her tongue. We soon got to the house, and as we walked toward the front door, we could hear yelling coming from inside.

Leon's voice rang through the door. "You think you're a man? I'ma beat yo' ass like a man!"

I looked at her. "What the hell?"

We rushed inside and saw Leon and Sean throwing blows. Leon was a grown man fighting a teenaged boy. But fortunately, my brother had the body of a grown man. He stood toe-to-toe with his ass and was giving him the business like Mike Tyson in his heyday. But the sight of him fighting my brother triggered me so instinctively that I flew into the fight too.

"Get the fuck off my brother!"

It felt like all of my pent-up pain and rage I'd been feeling for weeks finally exploded. I grabbed an umbrella from the side of the door and went upside his bald head with the handle. Leon turned around and glared at me.

"You little bitch!" He lunged toward me.

I avoided him. "Fuck you! I got yo' bitch!" I swung and cracked him again across the head. He shouldn't have taken his eyes off Sean, because he tackled him like a linebacker. Once he was on the floor, we both started giving him a beatdown. It felt good, both of us kicking his ass. *If you mess with one of us, you fight both of us.*

Next, we all heard the unbelievable. "Stop it now!"

We all paused and looked in shock at Mom because we'd never heard her that angry.

"Get the fuck out of my house!"

I was in shock. I thought this was the first time I'd ever heard her cuss.

Leon looked confused. "What? Baby, he came at me and—"

"I don't want to hear it! You attacked my son!" She shook her head. "I've been so scared of being alone that I've ignored everything you've done. That might make me a bad mother, but I'm not going to let you abuse my kids anymore. Get your shit and get out now."

"Baby, we need to talk about this first."

Leon walked toward her and touched her hand. Then she did the most gangsta thing I ever saw her do. She pimp slapped the shit out of him. Leon staggered backward, holding his face, and Sean and I looked at each other with amazement.

"Get out," she roared.

We both stood beside her.

"You heard her." I smirked. "Or do you want some more?"

Still holding his face, he said, "After everything I did for you, this is how you going to do me? Fine. You just lost the best thing you've ever had."

Leon marched out the front door.

My mother turned and looked at us. "You two are the best things in my life. I'm so sorry, Sean. Can you please forgive me?"

"I love you, Mom."

Sean gave her a hug. Then she hugged me. I couldn't believe my mom did that. She finally kicked Leon's ass out for good. *Just when I almost lost all respect for her, she goes and does this. Wow! I guess anything is possible.*

Later on that night, we ended up putting Leon's clothes in trash bags and tossed them outside. Trash pickup was in the morning.

Chapter Nineteen

Selfish

Nia Scott

Instagram and YouTube videos were my preferred forms of entertainment. They were my way of not thinking about my reality. Every now and then I would see something silly Brandon would post, and I would miss him even more. I wasn't having much success at forgetting about him.

I hadn't heard from him since we talked a couple of weeks ago, and maybe that was a good thing. Maybe he'd moved on. As much as I missed him, I couldn't see myself being back in Atlanta anytime soon. It'd be better for both of us if we just went our separate ways. On another note, my mother and Sean were becoming closer now that Leon was gone. She really surprised me by kicking him out. Even our relationship had improved.

As I was deep in thought, I heard the doorbell chime, so I got up and went downstairs. When I opened the door, I was thrown for a loop. I wanted to jump in his arms but run away at the same time. Even in a black bubble jacket and a Keffiyeh-style scarf and gloves, he still was shivering from the Chicago cold.

He smiled. "Hello, stranger."

"Brandon . . . hi. What are you doing here?"

"It's spring break."

"And you came here?" I couldn't contain my smile.

"I've heard great things about Chi-town."

"Un-huh, come in."

He walked inside and quickly closed the door behind him.

"Who is it, Nia?" Mom asked when she walked into the living room.

"It's my friend from school, Brandon."

He gave her a wide smile and extended his hand toward her. "Hello, it's nice to meet you, Mrs. Scott."

"Oh, please, call me Anna," she replied in a flirtatious tone.

Sean emerged from upstairs with his basketball in his hand.

"Sean, this is my friend, Brandon." I caught myself before I said "boyfriend." *Why did I do that?*

Brandon greeted him with the standard dap and man hug they all seemed to give each other.

"You must be the Rookie of the Year I've heard so much about."

Sean smiled and bounced the ball back and forth from hand to hand. "Ah, I see my legend precedes me."

"Can we get up on a game later?"

"You sure you want that? You already heard about me. Don't want to embarrass you."

"I won't go so hard on ya." Brandon shrugged and smiled at Sean.

"Oh, whatever, man." Sean chuckled. "You better bring yo' A game!"

"Let's give them some time together," my mother suggested to Sean.

"All right." He nodded. "Later, man."

Mom and Sean went back upstairs, and I settled on the couch next to Brandon. I stared at him, speechless. I still couldn't believe he came here to see me. "Where you staying?"

"I got an Airbnb downtown."

"Why didn't you tell me you were coming?"

"I wanted to surprise you."

"Well, you certainly did that."

He leaned in to kiss me. I pulled away and brushed my hair back from my face.

"You know, if I didn't know any better, I would think you aren't happy to see me."

"No, I am. It's just . . . I didn't think you would come here."

I looked away from him. He touched my chin and gazed into my eyes.

"You were wrong." He kissed me, and I fell in love all over again.

After a few minutes at my house, I drove Brandon to his Airbnb. I still couldn't believe he was here with me. I missed him so much. Even though I still felt guilty about everything that happened with Kyle, I didn't regret my feelings for Brandon. As I drove, I filled him in on what happened at home.

"Leon just went off like that? Wow. And your moms pimp slapped him?"

I laughed. "Like Bishop Don Juan himself. Believe me, I was more shocked than he was."

"I'm glad she came to her senses." He looked at me. "What about you?"

"What about me?"

He took my hand. "Have you come to your senses, or are you still trying to break up with me?"

I exhaled. "I was not breaking up with you. I just needed to sort things out."

"That's what it sounded like the last time we talked."

"I didn't want you to be waiting for me."

"Why don't you let me make that decision?" He smiled. "And I've decided that I won't let you get away that easy." Once we arrived at the Airbnb, he asked me to come inside. Truth was, he didn't have to ask me. I was going inside regardless. Being with him again gave me such an overwhelming rush of emotions, but I was also at peace. I cried as we made love. That was the first time that had ever happened. No matter how much I tried to push Brandon away, I knew if I saw him, I would give into him. And I gave him all of me. I needed his touch again. I needed to feel him. I felt him deep inside of me like he was trying to heal every wound I had in my soul. My orgasm washed over me, making me feel so good. Brandon was so gentle, so attentive, as he catered to my body's and soul's every desire, and for those few precious hours I forgot about the pain I'd been feeling inside for the past few months.

Afterward, I was lying in his arms, deep in thought. After all that shit I'd said about going our separate ways, as soon as I saw him, it was my legs that went their separate ways. Could we really just pick back up where we left off and be together again?

We spent the next few days secluded in what seemed like our own love cocoon. I'd never been this much in love with anybody in my life. I wished that were enough to ease my mind. I'd managed to avoid the topic I'd dreaded discussing, but I knew it would come up sooner or later.

"You sure you got everything?" I asked as he stuffed his duffle bag.

He glanced at me. "Everything except you."

"C'mon now," I sighed. "You still have me. Shit, you've had me any way you wanted since you've been here."

"That's not what I meant, and you know it. I want you to come back to school."

There it was. *Damn.*

"I'm not sure I'm even going back," I responded softly.

Brandon stopped packing and stared at me. "So you went from maybe fall to not at all."

"I've been thinking I should stay in Chicago. I didn't realize how much I missed home and my family until now."

Brandon looked at me, not believing a word I just said. "Really?"

"Yeah, I think this is the right decision."

"What about medical school?"

"I can finish medical school here."

"You know," he sighed, "I thought if I gave you some time, you would be able to deal with it, but I guess I was wrong."

"What are you talking about?"

"I'm talking about Kyle."

There it was. The sucker punch.

"I have dealt with it and moved on."

"That's why you're afraid to come back to Atlanta."

"I'm not afraid," I countered.

"I bet you weren't even planning to finish school at all."

"You're being ridiculous. I'm doing this for myself."

"No, you're doing this because you still feel responsible for his death."

"This isn't about Kyle or you. It's about what I want."

"You're right. This is about you throwing everything you worked your ass off for out the window over some guilt you shouldn't even have."

"Kyle killed himself after he found out about us, so who do you think pushed him over the edge? I should've seen it coming! I knew he was abusing his medication way before he killed himself! I should've been there for him, but no, I was too worried about school, too worried about my grades to bother to help him. And as soon as he showed me how much he needed me, what did I do? I broke up with him! We shouldn't have gotten together so soon. We shouldn't have gotten together at all!"

Tears rimmed my eyes, and I could no longer hold them back.

"Nia, Kyle was my best friend, and I loved him like a brother, but I saw his bullshit long before you knew him. Kyle loved being the center of attention. He had issues he didn't want to deal with. And you broke up with him not because you were selfish, but because if you didn't, he would have taken you down with him." He paused, then continued, "Kyle wasn't thinking about anybody but himself when he killed himself. He wasn't thinking about his family, his mom, his friends, or you."

"I can't go back there. Every time I close my eyes, I see him."

He put his arms around me and held me. "I know. I'll give you some space to think. I'll support whatever decision you make. Just remember, you can't stop living your life, Nia. You can't throw away all you've worked for. You know this."

Brandon left for Atlanta the next morning. He knew me better than I thought. Even though he was right, I still didn't know if I could put Kyle behind me that easily.

More thoughts were swirling around my mind while I sat at the kitchen table picking at my food. All I could think about was what Brandon said to me. He was right, but I needed to figure out my plan on my own.

My mother walked into the kitchen, glanced at me, then went in the fridge. She took out some frozen chicken to defrost for dinner later. She didn't say anything to me as she placed it in a bowl and set it on the counter. Then she sat next to me.

"I've been thinking about what you said the other day, Nia. I know I've never been the most supportive parent when it came to you going to medical school, but I was always proud of you."

I looked at her. "Really?"

"Yes. I may have given you my forehead," she joked, "but your drive came from your father. I was proud of your determination and commitment."

"So why were you so hard on me and my choice to become a doctor?"

"I . . . I just didn't want you to end up being alone like me."

"Mom, you're not alone."

"Yes, I am, Nia."

"Just having a male body around doesn't guarantee anything. The wrong one can bring more loneliness. You have to have the right one in order to add to your life. Look at you. You're a strong, independent, beautiful, and sexy woman. Any man would be happy to have you, Mom. Leon's dusty butt was the lucky one."

"Nia!" She blushed.

"It's true. You just lowered your standards with him."

"I get it, sweetheart. Thank you for that. I now see how happy you were about school, and I haven't seen that joy in you since you've been back. You know what else I see?"

"What, Mom?"

"I see that Brandon really cares about you."

"I know he does."

"Nia, don't take on the burden of Kyle's choice to end his life. Don't make the same choice and end yours by staying here. My daughter is a doctor. Remember that."

She got up and walked away. I never gave her enough credit. *I guess wonders never cease. For once my mom has my back.*

Chapter Twenty

Dorm Life

Nia Scott

Clark Atlanta (Summer Session)

It felt surreal being back. I still didn't know if I could do this, but I couldn't throw everything I worked so hard for out the window. I couldn't hold myself responsible for Kyle's death anymore. I'd never forget what happened, and I couldn't change the past, but like somebody told me, life goes on. As I was walking toward class, I saw a familiar face and squinted in disbelief.

"Sabina?"

She smiled. "Hey, Nia."

She looked totally different from before. She was dressed more reservedly in blue jeans and a simple black tee and had less makeup on. Her long black hair was flowing freely. To me she looked even more attractive.

"How are you?"

"I'm better than what I was." She shook her head. "I really want to apologize to you for what I did. I was so out of control. I don't blame you for kicking my ass out. I would have too."

I smiled. "I'm so glad to see you like this. What changed?"

"Well, I almost killed myself."

My eyes widened in shock. "You almost what?"

"Not deliberately, but I may as well have. I almost OD'd on Ecstasy."

"When did this happen?"

"A couple of months after I moved out. I moved in with Tony. I was so gone, partying every night. One night I collapsed in a club bathroom and woke up in the hospital. I checked myself into a rehab program. The first night I left rehab, I was back in the club and pretty soon doing the same thing over again. Then I heard what happened to Kyle." She paused for a moment. "It, um, it scared the hell out of me that someone I knew killed himself. I just remember thinking that if I didn't stop, I would be dead too. I've been clean for five months now. Looking back, I realize I've done a lot of foul things to the people close to me. I truly want to apologize to everybody I shitted on. My mom, my dad, and most of all you. I'm sorry, Nia."

I looked at her for a moment, then hugged her. After hearing everything that she went through, I couldn't help but feel sorry for her. "I'm glad you're doing better."

"I'm truly sorry for all the awful things I said to you."

"Don't worry about it. It's the past. If you ever need to talk, you know my number."

"Thank you." She smiled and walked away.

Kyle's death saved her life. How ironic was that? In a way it was like his death wasn't in vain.

It felt weird being here again, but it was where I wanted to be. I didn't tell Brandon I was back in Atlanta. I couldn't. I wanted to see him, but after the way we left things back in Chicago, and the fact that I'd never responded to any of his calls, texts, or even the invitation to his graduation, I was sure he'd moved on by now. For all he knew, I was still in Chicago feeling sorry for myself. All I did was push him away every time he tried to help me. I couldn't expect him to hold on forever. I wouldn't if I were him.

I signed up to take three classes this summer: Advanced Organic Chemistry, Primary Care Clerkship, and Chronic Illness Care. Instead of my own apartment, I decided to stay in CAU suites near campus. It worked out well because most of the students were gone and I was able to get a room by myself. It was a nice size, but it wasn't like having your own apartment.

For the first couple of weeks, I spent my time in class, studying, or sleeping. The dorms for the most part were like a ghost town, but that didn't mean it was empty. There was this one girl, Kima Rowe, a few doors down, who I talked to every now and then. She was real cool. Her boyfriend, Mike Sales, was a defensive tackle for the Georgia Bulldogs. She was also going to nursing school later in the fall. There was another girl, Michelle, across the hall, who I saw sometimes. She was a very attractive light-skinned sista who had naturally kinky hair. I heard her arguing with her boyfriend, Dorial, more than I saw her. Today, she was pissed because some girl named Adina kept texting Dorial, but he insisted he didn't know who she was. *I've been there before.* Their routine was arguing for an hour, then having makeup sex for another. How did I know? Well, let's just say Michelle was a very vocal girl in the heat of the moment. *Dorial must be laying that pipe down real good for her to put up with him and his shenanigans.*

Speaking of sex, I'd been tempted to call Brandon and let him know I was back. Would I sound too desperate if I told him to come over and check out my dorm? *Yes, that's a bit desperate sounding, but what if I text him? If he texts me back, cool.* I picked up my phone.

Hey. How are you? I'm back.

Not a minute went by before he responded.

Back in ATL?

I smiled and texted back.

Yeah, I'm in school.

Where are you?

I waited a minute before I responded. *Am I ready for this?* Then I heard Michelle and Dorial across the hall getting their ugly on.

I'm staying in the CAU suites.

Can I see you?

It was after midnight, and he wanted to see me. No doubt he wanted the same thing I wanted.

Where are you?

15 minutes away.

I jumped up off my bed and started straightening up my room. Then I texted him again.

Sure, come over. Room 218.

Okay.

Suddenly, butterflies hit my stomach, and I took off my sweatpants and T-shirt. I went in the dresser and pulled out my pink little boy shorts and matching tank top. I knew I brought them for a reason. Then I had to do a quick sniff test to see if everything was fresh. *Um, no, that will not do.* I ran to the bathroom, grabbed my washcloth, and gave myself a quick ho bath, hitting all the vital areas. *Whatever.* I brushed my hair and teeth, then sprayed some jasmine and vanilla body spray, and just like that I was Rooty Tooty Fresh & Fruity. Minutes later, I heard a knock on my door. *Damn, he must have flown over here.*

"Hey." I grinned from ear to ear when I opened the door. He was looking so damn good.

He bit his bottom lip as he looked me up and down, staring at me like I was a snack. "Hey, you." He hugged me, and butterflies took flight. He walked inside. "How come you didn't tell me you were back in town?" I closed the door. "I wanted to wait until the time was right."

"I missed you, Nia."

"I missed you too. I was kinda surprised to see that you were still in town. I thought you would've been back in Stone Mountain with your folks."

"I did go back for a minute, but I got a job downtown at Piedmont Health Care."

"What? That's great."

"What made you come back?"

"You and my mom did. You were right. I was running away from everything. This is where I should be." I could feel Brandon's eyes all over me.

"I hoped you would make the right decision. That's why I kept my distance."

"Well, I didn't call because I thought I finally pushed you away and you moved on." I looked at him. "Have you?"

We stared at each other in silence, and I thought we were both thinking the same thing. His smile. His lips. His eyes on my body like X-ray vision. Making me wet. I played with my hair and turned around to give him a better view of my ass. I wasn't like super thick, but I had a little something back there, especially when I arched my back. *These boy shorts ain't hiding much.* I felt Brandon's hands on my waist as he pulled me closer to him. His erection in his pants was pressing against me. Then I felt his warm, soft lips and faint breath on my neck. I could feel my heat becoming an inferno as he pulled down the shoulder straps on my top, exposing my breasts. His fingers caressed them as he went farther down my stomach and under my shorts. He touched me, and moans escaped my lips. His hands touched me in all the ways he knew I loved. I turned around and stared into his eyes.

"What do you want me to do?"

I bit my bottom lip. "Take off your clothes."

I sat back on my bed and watched him undress for me. *Damn, I just wanna lick him.* I reached out and touched his manhood. I massaged it in my hand, then took him into my mouth. This wasn't my first time going down on a man, but it wasn't something I did often. This was my first time doing this with Brandon. He'd never asked me for it, and I could tell he was surprised. He moaned softly as I licked, kissed, and sucked him into bliss.

I pulled him out of my mouth, looked up, and saw his eyes closed with a sheer look of satisfaction on his face. It turned me on knowing I did that. Suddenly, he picked me up and laid me on my back on my bed and returned the favor.

Now he'd given me head in the past, and it'd been good, but tonight he was on some other shit. I was feeling things that I never felt before. My breathing became choppy. I couldn't fight the feeling anymore and lost control. The sounds that left my mouth sounded like I caught the Holy Ghost. Brandon continued to eat me out even more vigorously.

"Oh, shit. Oh, shit . . ." I grabbed my sheets and anything I could get my hands on. I was flailing around on the bed, trying to handle this unbelievable feeling that washed over me. I was begging for mercy, but there was no pity for me tonight. Brandon was a warrior and was taking no prisoners. He finally came up for air and spread my legs. He entered me for the first time without a condom, and neither of us seemed to care. Sweet torture. He was in control. I was out of control. That scared and excited me at the same time.

He was marking his territory. Making me know daddy was home. Making my body sing. Making me cum. I was yelling all kinds of nasty shit. I needed this fuck. I needed to have my ass spanked. My hair pulled. I needed him just as bad as he wanted me. I could feel my wetness covering the bed beneath me. I had no choice but to sleep in the wet spot tonight.

"Oh, shit . . . gonna . . . cum . . ."

"Don't stop."

"Oh God . . . your shit feels so . . . good. No condom, Nia . . . I can't!"

"I don't care! Don't fuck it up!" What the hell was I saying?

"Nia . . . ah oh shit!"

He came and groaned like he'd just given me his all. I felt my vagina tremble again. It had been so long since I had a feeling like this that I almost forgot how good it was. We reveled in our orgasms for what seemed like hours before we fell asleep in each other's arms.

The next morning, I woke up with a big-ass smile on my face. Brandon was gone, but he'd left me a note saying that he went to IHOP to get breakfast. I lay in bed and thought about last night and giggled to myself. I finally managed to roll out of bed and put on a robe. I was sore, but it was a good sore.

I walked out of my dorm and saw Michelle walking toward her room. She gave me a funny look like I did something to her. I walked by her without saying a word. When I got to the showers, Kima had just gotten done taking one.

"Hey, girl," she greeted me in her deep New Orleans accent.

"Hey, Kima. What's wrong with Michelle?"

"Why? What did she do?"

"Nothing really, she just gave me this funny look in the hallway."

"Oh, well, I guess she didn't like the competition."

"Competition? What are you talking about?"

She grinned. "Well, it sounded like you had a hell of a good time last night."

My mouth dropped. "Oh, my God! You both heard me?"

"Girl, the whole damn building heard you. Your man must have put something awfully good on you last night," she joked.

I blushed from embarrassment, then nodded my head in acknowledgment.

"Well, go 'head wit' ya bad self!"

"What am I going to do about Michelle?"

Kima sucked her teeth. "Please, as much noise as that ho be making? She can't be saying anything!"

We laughed in unison because it was the truth. After I got done showering, I walked back to my room, and Brandon was waiting for me by my door with breakfast in his hand.

I walked up to him and give him a big French kiss. Michelle stepped out of her room and saw us. Brandon didn't notice her behind him. Once again she glared at me, shook her head, and kept going down the hallway.

I smiled. "Hey, you. It smells good."

"Come get some."

We went inside my room to eat breakfast. As we ate, Brandon kept glancing at me with a goofy grin on his face. "Nia, what made you, ah . . ."

"Go down on you?" I finished his question.

"Yeah. I mean, not that I minded, but you just never did before."

"I just really felt like it."

"Lucky me," he said and gave me a kiss.

That whole day in class, all I could think about was him. I was still having aftershocks from the orgasm, and my panties felt sticky. Just another reminder I needed to pick up that Plan B from CVS after class. I really should have been focused on class. I had an exam in three days, but all I could do was replay what happened last night. After I got what I needed at the pharmacy, I was walking back to my room and spotted Michelle, who mumbled something under her breath, and another girl with her, some skinny chick who glared at me.

"Ho," I heard in a low tone.

I turned around and looked at her. "Excuse me?"

The skinny girl spoke. "Aren't you that girl who used to date Kyle Hicks?"

I looked at her, surprised, then answered, "Yeah, why?"

"Didn't he blow his brains out because you were fucking his best friend?"

"What?" I was stunned.

Michelle chimed in, "Um hum, I guess you don't waste no time."

I wanted to punch her ass in the face, but that would have been stupid, especially with her buddy here. I turned and walked away. *After all this time, is that how people really see me?*

Chapter Twenty-one

The Ex Factor

Nia Scott

I decided to tell Brandon what Michelle and her ugly friend said to me earlier today. We were lying together on top of my bed. I still couldn't believe how they came at me like that. Brandon had some sound advice for me.

"Fuck them bitches."

"But is that what everybody who sees us together thinks?"

He shrugged his shoulders. "Who cares what people think? We know what really happened."

"I should have cussed out Michelle and her anorexic-looking friend!"

"Forget about it. She's just jealous because you got a good man."

"You're right. Her man is playing her for a fool."

"Sucks to be her, but let's not waste the night talking about them. I've been thinking about you all day."

"Me too." I turned over on top of him. "I was hoping for an encore."

He smiled. "I was waiting for you to ask."

Brandon gave me another mind-blowing experience. I didn't even try to control myself or keep the noise down. *If ol' girl has a problem, she better come say it to my face.*

A couple of days later, after class, I had some laundry to do and took a basket down to the laundry room. When I walked in, I saw Michelle's ass in there at the dryer. Part of me wanted to turn around and do my shit later, but fuck that. I wasn't going to let her bother me or run me away. I placed my basket down on top of the machine on the other side of the room and started to load my clothes. I acted like I didn't even see her. I guessed she was doing the same thing, but you know how some bitches are.

She walked over to me. "You sure have a lot more company over these days."

I glared at her. "Listen, you don't know me. And that bullshit you and your skinny-ass friend said to me was fucked up!"

"Bitch, please." She rolled her eyes. "You're the one fucking your dead boyfriend's best friend. That's what's fucked up!"

As she turned to walk away, it felt like something in my head snapped. I grabbed her by her hair and yanked her ass back toward me. "Say that shit again!"

Michelle flailed around trying to catch her balance as I dragged her ass to the floor. Luckily for her, Kima was walking by and heard the commotion.

"Hey! Stop it! Chill!" Kima grabbed me and pulled me off of her.

Michelle gathered herself off the floor and tried to charge at me. "Fuck you! I'ma whoop yo' ass, bitch!"

With open arms, I replied, "C'mon then!"

"No! Both of you stop it!" She stood between us. "Do you want to get kicked outta here?"

Michelle stopped in her tracks because Kima had a point. "This isn't over, bitch!"

"Bet," I shouted, ready for round two, and I charged at her.

"Oh, my God, c'mon," Kima said as she pulled me out of the laundry room. "Girl, have you lost your mind? You know what will happen if you two get caught fighting up in here."

"Nah, Kima, let me go She don't know me. She don't know what I've been through. She has no business talking to me like that."

"I know, I know! Listen, she's bugged out. But don't let her make you get kicked out of the dorm. She's mad because her man is trash and she knows it."

I exhaled. "Keep that bitch away from me."

"Okay, I totally understand. I'll bring your laundry to you, okay?"

I nodded. I was still pissed when I got back to my room. *That bitch better not even look in my direction when I see her or I'll crack her fucking skull.* It was bad enough I woke up every day and thought about Kyle's suicide. I didn't need that funky bitch throwing it in my face. Brandon was about the only person who eased that pain.

Thinking about everything again, I realized I couldn't stay here tonight, not this close to that bitch. After Kima brought my clothes to me, I took an Uber over to Brandon's apartment in College Park. He told me to stay for as long as I needed to. After I calmed down, I called Kima and thanked her for stopping me from making a huge mistake. Why risk everything I worked for because of her? I ended up staying at Brandon's place for a few nights before going back to the dorm.

A month went by relatively fine, with Michelle and me not acknowledging each other's existence. I found out from Kima that her bony friend's name was Tammy. I saw her every now and then, but she didn't say anything to me either. I would have stomped a mud hole in her skinny butt if she did.

The fall semester was right around the corner, and I passed all three of my classes. My relationship with Brandon got deeper each day that went by. It was like we knew one another on a deeper level. I'd never felt this way about anyone. Most of the time, I tended to want my space. You know how in relationships some guys get too possessive and don't give you breathing room? Brandon didn't do that. He knew when to give me space and time to myself, especially with school and needing time to study. Hell, I called him most of the time. As for my sex life, it was still crazy. He really knew how to calm my nerves after a rough day.

I got a call from Sabina a few weeks later, and she apologized for waiting so long to call me. She told me she was studying for classes, and I completely understood that. We finally caught up with each other on campus one day.

"I must have been crazy to take a full load of classes this semester! I should have taken a couple of them online."

"Nah, that's even more work. I did that one semester a few years ago and nearly lost my damn mind trying to keep up."

"Ugh." She looked at me. "On the real, thank you for giving me a second chance."

I smiled. "Sabina, you're not the only one who's ever made a mistake. The most important thing is you learned from it."

As we were walking on campus, I spotted Michelle and Tammy. They started pointing toward me. Up until now there was no further drama between us, but being that she was with her sidekick, Michelle might be feeling bold and shit. I decided to be cool and pay no attention to them. We walked by them, and once again the Olive Oyl–looking bitch whispered some slick shit under her breath.

"Bitch."

It took all of my willpower, but I ignored it. But Sabina hadn't quite reached my level of Zen. She turned around.

"Who you talking to?"

I touched her shoulder. "Forget it. Let's go."

"Ah, no! Why is she talking shit?"

Sabina stepped to them. Now Sabina was from the south side of Chicago, known for busting heads. Not only was Tammy skinny, but she was also petite. Sabina, at five foot six, towered over her. I could see that she didn't want no smoke with her.

Michelle spoke up. "I don't got no problem with you."

"If you got a problem with Nia, then you got one with me too!"

I pulled her back. As much as I would have enjoyed seeing Sabina kick her to sleep, I wasn't going to let her fight my battles or get in trouble.

I stared at Michelle. "I don't know what your problem is, but if you want to talk about it, we can. Or you can meet me off campus and we can do the other thing."

Michelle rolled her eyes and glanced at Tammy. "Let's go. I don't got time for this."

Sabina glanced at me. "What the hell was that about?"

"It's a long story."

I told Sabina over lunch what the confrontation was about, and she really wanted to kick Michelle's ass. It was funny seeing how eager she was to fight for me. Of course, I talked her down, but the more I thought about it, the more it didn't make sense for Michelle to be hating on me so much considering I didn't know her. The way she'd come at me was like a personal vendetta about Kyle's death and Brandon and me being together, but why?

Brandon suggested we spend the weekend at his apartment. I was fine with that and glad to get away from it all. Friday night, we went to Movies ATL at Camp Creek.

After the movie, we were driving through the Camp Creek Market Place to Panda Express.

"Sean called me last night. He wanted me to ask you if your game was still weak."

"What? I was getting mine! Anyway, he's good?"

I laughed. "Yeah, he's fine. My mother and he are doing better."

"You guys have been through a lot this year."

"Yeah, but I think the worst is over. Things seem like they're going . . . Oh, c'mon, this bitch?"

"What's wrong?"

We pulled into the parking lot, and I saw Michelle sitting outside of Panda Express with Dorial.

"Oh, my God, why is this bitch here!"

"Who?" Brandon looked around.

"Michelle!"

Brandon stared at her for a second.

"Come on, let's go!"

"Wait a minute, that's Brii."

"Brii? What are you talking about? That's Michelle."

"Damn, it makes sense now."

"What makes sense?" I crossed my arms and waited for an answer. "You know this ho?"

"It's not even like that. Brii Michelle. She has one of them double first names."

I looked at him like he was crazy. "How do you know?"

"Kyle used to call her Brii."

"Oh, my God."

"Yeah, as a matter of fact, he broke up with her to get with you."

"Are you serious?" I looked at her, then back at Brandon. "That's why this bitch has been acting stank. She was the one who was texting Kyle that night."

We pulled off the lot and went to another restaurant.

So this really isn't about Kyle killing himself. It's because he broke up with her to be with me. This chick got me fucked up!

A few days went by, and I was in my room studying for another exam. I got up and went downstairs to the lobby to get a Coke and Fritos from the vending machine. When I walked in, I spotted Dorial. I didn't acknowledge him, but I felt his eyes on my ass as I bent down to get my soda. I stood up and moved over to the snack machine. The Fritos dropped down, and out of the corner of my eye I spotted Michelle walking into the lobby wearing boy shorts and a pink T-shirt. Dorial was still gazing at my ass. He hadn't noticed Michelle yet, so I decided to get a little payback. I bent over slowly and pushed my ass up in the air. Dorial grunted and Michelle saw him.

She snapped, "What the fuck!"

Bingo.

He stuttered, "What? Nothing. I'm waiting for you."

"You were staring at that bitch's ass!"

I turned around. "Michelle, don't worry about it. I got a man. Besides, it's not like I'm going to take your boyfriend away from you . . . again."

Dorial looked confused. "Again?"

"Oh, yeah." I chuckled. "My ex-boyfriend, Kyle, dumped her for me. She's been hating on me ever since."

"Shut up, bitch!" Michelle yelled.

"Relax. It's not my fault your men can't stop looking at me. Y'all be safe now."

I sashayed back upstairs.

Coke: fifty cents.

Fritos: seventy-five cents.

Making Michelle look like a silly ho in front of her boyfriend . . . priceless.

Chapter Twenty-two

End of the Road

Nia Scott

In the beginning, things seem so far away that you barely think about them. But then, all of a sudden, it's here right around the corner. I was one month away from fall graduation and couldn't believe it. After everything I'd been through in the past four and a half years, I knew that this was only the beginning.

Final exams were here, and everybody was focused. Well, maybe not everybody. Michelle and Dorial had been going at it lately like cats and dogs. It was hard to concentrate on studying when I was too busy eavesdropping. Yeah, it was wrong for me to be listening to their business, but after all the shit she came at me with, I loved that she was miserable with her dude. I wished I could say they were fighting because Dorial was still staring at me, but that wasn't the case.

Kima stopped by my room. "Hey, girl, what's going on over there?"

"Well," I said as a sly grin spread across my face, "it sounds like the rumors have gotten back to Michelle that Dorial has been humping a lot of freshmen over at Spelman."

She raised her eyebrows, affirming what she knew. "She's just now hearing about it? That fool has been dogging her out since day one!"

"Really?"

"Michelle shoulda broken up with him a long time ago."

"I wish I could say I feel sorry for her, but I don't."

Kima looked at me seriously. "Nia, not that you need my approval or anything, but I don't feel like you're doing anything wrong being with Brandon. If you find somebody you really have a connection with, then you should do everything in your power to be with them."

"Thanks for saying that. I was starting to believe everybody here saw me as a slut or something."

Kima huffed. "Girl, the only ho here is across the hall!"

The next day I was coming in from class, walking up to my room, and I saw Dorial and Michelle kissing in the hallway. I guessed the sex was stronger than the truth. After they were done sucking face, Dorial walked by me with a smirk on his face, lustfully but discreetly looking me up and down. I rolled my eyes. Michelle stood at her door, glaring at me like I wanted to jump on her man and dry hump him or something.

She smirked. "I know you wish you had a man like mine."

I chuckled. "You can keep your man. He don't got nothing to offer me."

"Um hmm."

Before I opened my door, I turned and looked at her. "Michelle, I don't care if you like me. That's your business. But all this bullshit you been coming at me with over Kyle is silly. Kyle made a choice to take his life, and that had nothing to do with me. I tried to get him help, but he didn't want it. I was not responsible for his life."

"Say whatever you want, but if Kyle had been with me, he wouldn't have killed himself."

I shook my head. "You know, you could be right. We'll never know what could have happened. But the fact is that Kyle had problems he didn't want to or didn't know how to deal with. He killed himself right in front of me. I held him as he bled in my arms. I had to call his mother and tell her that her son blew his brains out, so don't tell me what you coulda done or what woulda happened if you had been with him. As far as I'm concerned, I did you a favor."

Michelle was speechless. I turned and went inside my room. *I guess the truth will set you free.*

I invited Brandon over later that night to share with him the news I received earlier in the day about med school. Even though I would have to wait until next July to start, I was still happy to get in. He hugged me with excitement and offered sincere words of encouragement and happiness. He was my own personal cheering squad, always telling me to follow my dreams.

"I'm so happy for you. This is what you wanted."

I smiled. "Yeah, but it's not the only thing I want."

He grinned. "Oh, you gonna get that too, but I also wanted to tell you something."

"What?"

"I don't know what the future is going to be like for us with the distance, but I do know I want to be with you."

"I want to be with you too."

"So do you think we should take that next step? Not saying we need to, but how do you feel about us living together?"

"Brandon," I exhaled, "you know how I feel about you, but it's a big step. I mean, we spend a lot of time together as it is, but . . ."

"I know it's a big step. Take your time and mull it over. Whatever decision you make, I'm cool with."

I stared into his brown eyes and kissed him. *Brandon is amazing. What girl wouldn't want to be with him?* It wasn't the same when Kyle wanted us to move in together. I just wanted to make sure I was making the right decision. We were on the same page in every way that mattered. *I'll make my decision after finals.*

Sabina called me and told me that she passed her finals. To think, just a year ago I couldn't stand the girl, and now here I was extremely proud of her. She went from a full-on party girl, a damn near strung-out porn star, to an exemplary student. The judgment of people took a toll on her at times, but she never succumbed to it. Sabina was a living example that you can beat your inner demons.

As for Michelle, she finally wised up and dumped Dorial. Maybe finding him in bed with Tammy helped her see the light. Apparently, Tammy had been sucking Dorial off all summer. *I guess that's what friends are for.* Michelle not only dumped Dorial but also kicked Tammy's ass up and down the street. Michelle didn't have anything else to say to me after we had our little talk in the hallway.

My mother and Sean called and told me they would be flying down with my dad for my graduation. I was surprised they all would be traveling together. My relationship with my mother was one I never thought I'd have with her. I told her about the talk Brandon and I had, and she simply told me to follow my heart. I didn't think I would ever get over what Kyle did, but it made me stronger.

My graduation ceremony was being held at the Jefferson Academic Center. It was huge, with stadium-like seating filled with my fellow classmates in black robes. There was a buzz and excitement in the air as people posed for pictures, laughed, and hugged each other. My parents greeted me with a hug while Sean took pictures of us together as a family. It was weird because it had been so long since we were all together like this. My mother and father seemed very friendly toward one another. If I didn't know any better, I would have thought they were still married, but I knew this was just a happy time for all of us.

The ceremony started, and of course there was the great valedictory speech, but the one that blew me away was the commencement address by Michelle Obama. I never felt more inspired by a woman in my life. Seeing her in person was incredible. Soon after, the dean began calling out names, and students were walking up and receiving their degrees. It felt like forever for him to get to the S's and say my last name, but when he did, I felt an eruption of joy inside me.

"Nia Scott."

I walked up to the dean, shook his hand, and took my degree. I turned and looked to the side and saw a familiar face and smiled. I walked off the stage while my family was cheering the loudest for me. After the ceremony, I found them in the crowd of people.

My father, Jeffery Scott, was a handsome man. Both Sean and I got our height from him. He stood at six foot four and had deep mocha skin and pretty brown eyes. My father's deep baritone voice always made me feel safe.

He hugged me. "I'm proud of you, baby girl."

"Thanks, Dad."

Sean added with a smile on his face, "I knew you could do it."

"Thank you, Sean. Now all we have to do is get you here."

"All right. You going to hold me down?" he asked.

"Don't I always?"

My mom took my hand as tears rimmed her eyes. "I'm so proud to call you my daughter."

I felt a swell of emotions I never thought I would feel for my mother. Despite all the drama, I always wanted her to be proud of me. Tears ran down my face. "I'm proud to be your daughter."

We hugged for what felt like the first time ever. After a few minutes of taking more pictures, I spotted somebody coming my way who I wanted to thank as well. "I'll be right back."

"Okay, baby." Mom nodded.

Dad's eyes narrowed. "Who's that?"

My mother giggled. "Later, Jeff."

As for Brandon, he'd had my back no matter what. Love was love. It hadn't changed, only grown, and so had my feelings for him.

"You were late."

"I got held up at work, but I saw you walk. I told you I'd be here."

"I never doubted it."

He hugged me. "How do you feel?"

"Like I wouldn't be here without you."

"Nah, you did this all by yourself. I just kept you company."

"Do you remember the thing you asked me about the other day?"

"Yeah, I do."

"Yes. I want to live with you."

A big smile spread across his face, and he kissed me like it was our wedding day. I was sure my dad was going to want to have a word or two about this, but I guessed I was finally taking my mother's advice to follow my heart.

Ten Years Later

Chapter Twenty-three

I Wasn't Ready

Nia Scott

Chicago

It's funny what you think your life is going to be and what really happens. It was the eve of a new year, and everything I thought I knew was going to change.

Brandon and I were in a nightclub, celebrating the end of the year and looking forward to an even better new year. I was an emergency attending at Grady, and it was going extremely well. I had many offers from quite a few health systems, but I accepted the one closest to my heart. Brandon was a guidance counselor and head varsity basketball coach at South Atlanta High School. His connection and commitment to his students earned him Counselor Educator of the Year by the Georgia School Counselor Association (GSCA). I was so proud of everything he had accomplished over the years.

We were spending the holiday in Chicago and staying with my mother. Sean was also in town and staying at our mom's. I was so proud that he fulfilled his dreams and was drafted from Grambling State University and was a starting guard in the NBA. He had all sorts of women throwing ass at him left and right. Why did he have to be so cute? I constantly warned him not to get any of those little groupies pregnant. I hoped he would listen to me.

"Ten, nine, eight, seven, six, five, four, three, two, one. Happy New Year," we all yelled, and Brandon kissed me. I couldn't believe how happy we still were together.

"I love you, Nia Scott."

"I love you too, Brandon Griffin."

"I can't believe how beautiful you look tonight." Brandon looked at me in awe.

"Thank you."

Despite how cold it was outside, I still had on only a silver strapless dress, and Dolce & Gabbana pumps to match, with my hair in an updo. We drank and danced until three in the morning.

We were heading back to my mother's. I didn't know what it was, but after a night of drinking, my hormones were on overdrive. I was feening for penis right about now, but my old-school mother made sure Brandon and I slept in separate rooms while we were there. I mean, she knew Brandon and I had been living together for years now, so what the hell did she think we'd been doing?

Our Uber driver pulled up to the front of the house around three thirty, and Brandon helped me out. As I wobbled up the driveway toward the door, I just wanted to bite him. He was looking so delectable.

"Do you know . . . what I wanna do to you?" My words slurred.

He grinned. "Yeah, but we can't in your mother's house."

"I know, but we're not in the house right now." I gestured to the side of the house.

"Oh, hell no. Baby, it's freezing out here, and you're drunk. I'm not getting frostbite on my joint."

I grabbed at his crotch. "But I'm horny!"

"Yeah, horny, got it." He moved my hands. "We can wait."

I wrapped my arms around him and dry humped his leg. "I don't wanna wait! I want you to bang me . . . like . . . like . . . how you . . . bang . . ."

"Come on. Let's go inside."

I whined, "But, baby . . ."

"Come on."

"I'm not your friend."

Brandon took the house keys out of his pocket and opened the door. I staggered into the darkness, bumping the side table. Brandon stared at me and shook his head. As we went farther inside, we heard a faint moan coming from downstairs.

"What's that noise?"

"It sounds like a girl."

"Did Sean come home?" Brandon asked.

"I'm gonna kill his ass if he's fucking some ho in here! If I can't get some, he damn sure can't!"

I took off my shoes so I wouldn't fall creeping down the stairs. The moans got louder, and I got madder. Each moan was preceded by a thump. No doubt what that was. I swore I was going to kill my brother. We tiptoed toward the bedroom, and I flipped on the lights.

"Sean, I'ma—"

I froze. I wished I never saw what I did.

"Oh, my God . . . Mom?"

I saw my mother's face looking up at me. She was lying on her back with her legs resting on the shoulders of some man banging her back in.

"Nia! Oh God . . . Jeff, get off me!"

My jaw dropped to the ground. "Dad?"

He scrambled to cover them with the sheets, but I was already scarred for life.

Brandon pulled me away from the room. "Nia, I think we should leave."

I was glad I was drunk. I wanted to forget this forever!

Later that morning, after I sobered up and was able to deal with what I saw a few hours ago, it was time to have a talk with my parents. Inwardly, I was elated they were back together, but trying to forget the image of them getting their ugly on required a shot of Patrón.

We sat at the kitchen table together over breakfast.

"How long has this been going on?" I glared at both of them.

"Well, your father and I have been talking to each other again for a while now."

I gave her the side-eye. "Talking? I know talking when I see it, and you two were definitely not talking last night."

My father tried to suppress a grin, then took her hand. "Honey, your mother and I have a lot of history together."

I rolled my eyes when their fingers interlocked. "I get that, but why didn't you both try to fix it before getting divorced?"

"We tried. We were young when we got married and didn't know what it took to make a marriage work. Instead of communicating, we talked at each other, and neither of us listened. We couldn't agree on anything, and we began to drift apart."

"Okay, so why after all this time being divorced did you two decide to . . . ugh!" I grimaced at the memory of what I saw.

"Nia, it wasn't like that," Mom clarified. "We still love each other, and we're grown."

"Oh, okay, cool. Oh, by the way, this whole 'sleeping in separate rooms' thing you've been making Brandon and me do is so out the window."

She exhaled. "No, it's not. We were married."

"*Were* married," I repeated. "You two aren't married now."

"That's not the point." Mom looked at my dad. "Jeff, say something."

He laughed. "Baby girl, when you graduated from Clark, your mom and I kept in contact. A lot of the things we had problems with years ago aren't problems anymore. We never stopped loving each other. We just realized that we had problems and we couldn't live together."

I looked at both of them. "What you two are saying is that when Sean and I needed you to be around for us, you two were on a break. Now that we're both grown, it's all good? Okay."

"Honey, you know it's not like that. It would have been worse for your mother and me to stay together and be fighting like cats and dogs in front of you and Sean."

Sean came downstairs with Brandon behind him. "Hey, Dad, what are you doing here?"

I looked at him. "He's hooking up with Mom on the low."

"Nia!" My mom was embarrassed.

His eyes widened like saucers. "Really? Damn. How long y'all been creeping?"

My mother touched her brow. "We were not creeping, we wanted to keep this to ourselves for a while."

"A while? Almost ten years is more than a while. I caught them getting their freak on downstairs last night."

My mother groaned, mortified.

"Oh, snap!" Sean laughed hysterically. "Pops, you da man!"

Brandon placed his hand on my shoulder. "Nia, I need to talk to you."

"It can wait."

Brandon took my hand. "No, it can't. Excuse us please." Once we were out of earshot, I let go of his hand. "What is it?"

"Why are you being so hard on your parents? C'mon, they're grown."

I folded my arms. "Yeah, grown people having a booty call in the back room."

"Why are you tripping? Sean seems to be very happy about this."

"Sean was a kid when they divorced. He's wanted them back together since day one. He wasn't old enough to understand."

"Well, you're thirty-two years old now. I think you're old enough to act like an adult about this instead of like an angry teenager."

Okay, ouch. That one hurt, but I did have it coming. That was one of the things I loved about Brandon—he was never afraid to call me on my bullshit. But it really bothered me for some reason that my mother and father were together again now that we were adults but couldn't keep it together for us when Sean and I were kids.

Later that night, we all sat down and had dinner together as a family. The more I thought about it, I began to put all the pieces together. Over the years when my residency and fellowship would allow, I would come home, and my dad would come over to visit me. I didn't doubt that was true, but obviously he was here to see Mom, too. It didn't click because I simply enjoyed us being together.

After dinner, I wanted to talk to my dad alone to find out what the deal was for real. We had a seat in the living room.

"Dad, why didn't you just tell me?"

"Nia, I feel like your mother and I have put you and your brother through so much pain. Besides, we've only really been seeing each other for two years."

"Only two years? Well, that makes it better." I rolled my eyes. "Is it going to work this time?"

He smiled. "I think so. We don't want to make the same mistakes again."

"I understand."

"How have you been? How are things in the ER?"

"Things can't be any better. The ER is different every day. Some days are more challenging than others, but I wouldn't change it for anything. You always told me I could do it, Dad, and I did."

"You did, baby girl. I'm so proud of you." He paused momentarily and spoke again. "How are things with you and Brandon?"

"We're good. Really happy together. Everything has come full circle."

"I'm glad. That's all I really wanted for you, to be happy."

Sean walked in, sat next to me on the couch, and leaned his oversized self on me.

"Boy, get your heavy butt off me!" I shoved him.

He pulled me closer, kissed my forehead, and put his arm around me.

"I don't know who you been touching and kissing on down in North Carolina. I ain't trying to catch nothing."

"I told you I'm careful."

"It doesn't matter how careful you are," Dad interjected. "These young girls will try to trap you."

"I know. That's why I mess with the older ones." Sean looked at us both with a shit-eating grin.

Dad couldn't suppress his laugh at Sean's antics, but I popped him.

"So, Dad, you going to move back in?"

"I don't know yet. Maybe."

"Might as well. Besides, I might have to use the guest room later. Got these twins coming by."

My dad chortled.

I shook my head and stood up. "Oh, my God. I'm going to bed."

Sean smirked. "Whose bed?"

He thinks his ass is slick trying to put me on the spot in front of Dad. "The same bed my man is sleeping in. Good night!"

Chapter Twenty-four

Diagnosing the Idiot

Nia Scott

Atlanta

The ER was incredibly slow this particular morning, so I made a quick run to the floor to visit an old friend of mine from college, Kima, who was scheduled to have a small bowel resection tomorrow morning.

"How are you feeling?"

She smiled nervously. "Scared as hell. Somebody is about to cut me open tomorrow."

"I understand. This is typical with everything you've been through with Crohn's though," I reassured her. "Who's your surgeon?"

"A Dr. Armstrong. Do you know him?"

"Ahh." I nodded my head. "You'll be just fine. He's one of the best."

"If you say so. I'd still rather put my life in your hands."

I smiled. "Surgery isn't my specialty, but if you're ever in a car accident, I gotcha."

"I'll make sure you're the first one I call," she responded jokingly.

Just as we were catching up, the devil himself walked into the room. He didn't even acknowledge Kima but instead looked around, then glared at me. Mark and I had known each other for years, and we really didn't like each other at all.

"Dr. Scott, what are you doing here? Are you moonlighting as a real doctor instead of supplying Band-Aids to attention seekers?"

"Wow." I rolled my eyes. "You're even less funny than I remembered. Actually, I'm visiting my friend, who you're operating on tomorrow, and I told her that you're the best at your job."

"Well, that part you got right. I am the best."

I narrowed my eyes, then looked at Kima. "I'm going back to the ER, but if you need—"

"Why would she need you?" He looked at me. "What do you know about any type of surgery?"

"If you didn't so rudely interrupt me, I was telling my friend she can call me anytime if she needed anything."

"Good. As long as we're clear as to who's the expert here."

Kima watched the exchange, and I could see the concern in her face.

"Dr. Armstrong, may I have a word with you?" I gestured toward the hallway. I was so tired of the disrespect from White men who were intimidated by a Black woman's success. We both had MD behind our names.

Once we were out of the room, I started in. "What is your problem?" I looked at him intently. "I'm telling my friend, who is afraid of being cut on, that you're the best, and you come at me like an asshole!"

Instantly, his ears turned bright red. "Relax, Dr. Scott, I . . . I was just joking," he lied.

"Joking my ass. It's no secret we don't like one another, Mark, but you really need to keep whatever issues you have with me out of your bedside manner. If that were me in that room and I saw how you treated a colleague, especially a female colleague, I'd request a second opinion simply because I'm female. My thoughts would be, 'If he's treating her like that, will he really take care of me?' Let's not even bring up the issue of race and disparities of care given to Black women."

Like the privileged person he was deemed by societal standards, he looked like he was about to blow. His face matched his ears, and he was visibly annoyed by what I said. "Your friend is in good hands," he repeated. "I'd just appreciate you letting me do my job and letting me explain to my patient what's going on."

I looked at him and saw he was really trying to find something else condescending to say, and I was ready for it. I really wanted to tell him to kiss my black ass, but instead, I took the high road.

"When you understand I wasn't trying to do your job, you will be more effective at your job. Now excuse me while I say goodbye to my friend so I can go and Band-Aid more attention seekers."

He huffed and marched away. I rolled my eyes and walked back inside the room.

"That arrogant son of a bitch is going to do my surgery?" Kima quizzed. "He's an asshole."

"Girl, I'm sorry you had to see any of that. I'm sure you won't see that side of him again."

"I respect you saying that, but you know he ain't shit, and you know I will fuck him up. He'll need more than a damn Band-Aid."

I couldn't help but laugh at Kima's blunt ass. He always tried to use his reputation to intimidate and bully his peers, but he wasn't going to get away with that bullshit with me. Not then and damn sure not now.

When I returned to the ER, I walked into the doctors' break room, where our two newest doctors were sitting at a table. Dr. Anthony Kelly, a second-year resident, was smart and very proficient in his work, but from my observation, he lacked the people skills needed when dealing with patients. Dr. Jayla Spencer, an intelligent Black woman who was a second-year fellow, was only a few months away from graduation and becoming an attending. She was also bright and talented. She was the total opposite of Dr. Kelly. She had a gentle soul and showed a level of empathy I rarely saw in any of the other residents or fellows who rotated through the ER.

We all worked together and tended to patients, clearing the board. When I was in school, I never really thought of the patients much. I guessed in school I saw them as being different cases and ailments but not as real people with needs and feelings. I was surprised at times how ignorant some people could be. For example, Mr. Herbert Grey from Roswell was a 74-year-old hard-core bigot who often used the ER as a doctor's office.

Later that day, I saw that Jayla was assessing him, so I stepped inside the room to make sure things didn't get out of hand.

"Mr. Grey, what brings you here today?" Jayla inquired.

He frowned. "Where's my doctor at?"

"Sir, I am your doctor."

He flared his nostrils like a bull about to blow. "No, you aren't. Where's the tall, blond-haired, blue-eyed, competent man I've seen before?"

She immediately knew who he was referencing. "Sir, Dr. Claremont isn't here today, but I can help you."

"I want to see my doctor! He knows exactly what my condition is!"

She forced a smile. "Well, sir, if you tell me what's wrong, I'm sure I can help you."

"Just call my doctor!"

"Mr. Grey, as I mentioned, Dr. Claremont is not here, but I'm more than glad to help you."

"I don't want a colored girl touching me!"

And there it was. Mr. Grey and his true colors shining brightly.

I noticed that Jayla was taken aback and didn't know what to say. Part of me wanted to laugh at him because I didn't think anybody said "colored" anymore. After dealing with Mark earlier and now this fool, a part of me wanted to bust his old ass upside his head. I could only imagine how Jayla felt. I decided to step in before the situation escalated.

I pulled up his chart and looked over his history. Dr. Claremont normally ordered a cortisone shot for his rotator cuff injury.

"Okay, Mr. Grey, we will find someone who can help you."

I glanced at the feeble old man, held back a laugh, then stepped out of the room with Jayla.

She looked at me. "In my head I knew what I wanted to say, but if I had said it, it would bring on more problems because it wouldn't have been nice."

"I completely understand. You handled that situation as well as you could."

She exhaled. "Had I been in my first or second year of residency, that situation probably would have gone left."

I chuckled. "Just so you know, you're one of the best doctors who has rotated on this service in a while."

"Thank you, Dr. Scott."

"Keep up the good work."

I had to admit it felt really good going home. My mind and body were tired. Brandon typically got home after

I did, depending on my shift. We recently moved into a four-bedroom house in Decatur. It would have been great if we'd ever gotten to spend time here together. Since we'd gotten back from Chicago it had been nonstop. I pulled out my cell and checked my messages.

"Hey, girl, I know you're working your ass off, but remember we're going out to dinner tomorrow night. I can't wait for you to meet Jon. Anyhoo, call me when you get this. Love ya, bye."

Sabina, the girl who drove me crazy in college, had been my best friend for years now. She'd matured and grown into a woman. Although, in my opinion, her taste in men was still questionable, I decided to give this new guy a chance and made a mental note to call her later.

After a quick shower, I lay down in my bed and fell asleep. A few hours later, I felt something pulling my clothes off. At first I thought I was dreaming, but then I opened my eyes and saw Brandon carefully sliding my panties off me.

I smiled. "What do you think you're doing, Mr. Griffin?"

He spread my thighs apart. "Well, you looked very uncomfortable with these on. I thought maybe you'd feel better with them off."

"Well, I trust your judgment, Counselor."

I leaned my head back on my pillow and released some built-up tension. My legs couldn't stop shaking. *I swear, he should be a gynecologist the way he knows my vagina.*

The next night, Brandon and I met Sabina and her friend, Jon, at Chili's at Camp Creek for dinner. She had only been seeing this guy for a couple of months, but this was the first time we went out as couples. He seemed friendly enough. Easy on the eyes: dark hair, blue eyes, and a nice tan. Sabina had always been an equal-opportunity dater. She liked all types of men.

We were at the table talking over drinks. I leaned in. "Jon, what do you do?"

"I'm a loan officer with Bank of America, but my passion is acting."

"Oh, okay, film or TV?"

"I've gotten small roles on a few CW shows, but mostly plays."

Sabina smiled. "Yeah, I saw him in a play at the Fox and met him afterward. We stayed in contact with each other ever since."

"Well, how could I let a woman as beautiful as her get away?" He took her hand. "So you two have been friends since college?"

"Yeah, we used to be roommates."

Sabina laughed. "I used to drive her crazy."

Jon smiled. "Really? You got stories?"

"We've been through some things."

She shook her head. "Thank God I'm past that phase in my life."

Brandon snickered. "Yeah, you were something else. There were times I thought I was going to come over and see Nia choking you."

"Oh, now you gotta tell me more! What did she do?" Jon looked at the three of us.

Sabina laughed. "Nothing! I was just misunderstood."

I stared at her matter-of-factly. "Misunderstood? Oh, is that what we're calling it? Don't make me go there."

She shook her head. "Will I ever hear the end of that?"

"Nope!" The three of us had a good laugh.

"Remember that time we went to the club and you left me there for some other dude?" Brandon chimed in with embarrassment from the memory.

"Really, Brandon? You were just standing there doing nothing!" She rolled her eyes. "You were boring."

"I was trying to dance with you, but you were doing the most! Not everything needs to be streamed live."

Jon smiled. "Wow, you two dated?"

Brandon couldn't contain his laughter. "Dated? No, we just went out once."

Sabina concurred.

We spent the rest of the night drinking, eating, and telling stories. I could tell Sabina was really feeling Jon. He was the total opposite of the kind of guys she dated in college. He was very attentive to her and knew how to hold a conversation. It was about time she found a good man.

Chapter Twenty-five

Code Blue

Nia Scott

Coffee and 5-hour Energy drinks had become my regular diet these days. Due to a snowstorm, we were extremely slow. Dr. DeJesus and I were the only attendings, and I was able to observe Jayla and Anthony with the few patients we had in our pod. We were in a room, speaking with a patient.

Jayla smiled. "Okay, ma'am, we're going to give you some antibiotics to fight the infection. Are you allergic to anything?"

"No, not that I know of. Will I have to stay here overnight?"

"No, ma'am. We'll give you IV antibiotics first. I'm going to write a prescription for the remainder of the treatment, and you should be fine. If you can just try to stay indoors for a couple of days and rest, you'll be as good as new."

She nodded. "Okay, thank you."

"You're welcome."

We exited the room and headed back to the physician's hub.

"Your bedside manner is so touching," Anthony said to Jayla in a sarcastic tone.

I was consulting with Dr. DeJesus on one of her patients but stayed close in case things went too far.

Jayla shook her head. "Well, one of us has to have some type of compassion."

"We could've been in and out of the patient's room two minutes ago. Just give her the diagnosis and treatment plan and keep it moving."

As smart as Anthony was, his arrogant attitude made being around him annoying.

Jayla stared at him, irritated. "She needed someone to listen to her. You couldn't tell that?"

"It's not my job to be her emotional support system. It's our job to diagnose and treat."

Jayla looked back at him and, once again, shook her head. "I did that and treated her like a human being all at the same time." Jayla rolled her eyes. "It's amazing how I can do both."

Anthony cut his eyes at her. "Don't think I don't know what you're trying to do."

"I'm trying to do my job and give my patients the best possible care I can."

"Whatever! You're trying to show me up in front of Dr. Scott. At the end of the day, it doesn't matter how nice a person you are. If you don't know the job, you're not going to be around for long."

She frowned and didn't back down. "I know my job. That's why I was able to diagnose and treat her. Why don't you worry about growing a personality people want to be around?"

"Don't think because you're Dr. Scott's favorite that you can talk to me any kind of way."

"What? Dr. Scott likes me because I'm a nice person and I'm good at my—"

"Excuse me?" he interrupted angrily. "I'm at the top of our class."

"Don't interrupt me," Jayla demanded forcefully. "Book smarts mean nothing if you have no compassion for people. You're a jerk. If you took the time to listen to somebody else instead of assuming you know it all, you might learn something."

She turned and walked away from him. In this world there was always going to be a man who would be threatened by our intelligence or skill. We simply had to stand our ground. Needless to say, I saw a lot of myself in her, and I was glad she didn't back down.

Jayla and Anthony didn't have any other conflicts that I saw after she put him in his place. The patient flow was steady. Just when I thought we were going to get through the shift pain free, chaos broke loose.

Our pagers went off three consecutive times: trauma stat: MVA. ETA: five minutes.

"What happened?" Dr. DeJesus asked someone in the comm center.

"There was a six-car pileup on I-85 North near exit 248B. We've got four patients inbound, and I anticipate more."

I looked at Jayla and Anthony. "Okay, we need trauma teams in rooms one, two, and three, stat! Can you two handle room four?"

"Yeah, we got it," Jayla said confidently.

We all had some level of fear of the unknown, but we were able to control it and do our jobs. Lives were in jeopardy.

The next four minutes flew by like they were on crack, and then the paramedics came crashing through the doors.

I looked at a medic. "What do we have?"

"Male: Jack Carey, thirty-eight, driver, side impact. He has internal bleeding. Bone exposed on left shoulder."

"Okay," I yelled, "exam room one, type and cross match!"

"Where's a suture pack? We got a bleeder here," another medic yelled.

Dr. DeJesus looked at the patient. "Keep pressure on the wound!"

"Are you running room four?"

She replied, "Yeah, what do you have?"

"Black male, twenty. His breathing is shallow."

"Okay, let's put in a chest tube."

"Okay!"

"Pressure's crashing, pulse is thready, respiration intermittent." Nurse Brown yelled, "His heart stopped!"

I looked at her. "I'm starting chest compressions. Somebody grab Dr. DeJesus, now!" I rushed toward them and took over the situation. "Code blue!"

Nurse Brown went into room one. I started compressions. There was so much chaos around me, I had to focus. "Three, one thousand, four, one thousand, five, one thousand . . ." I called out. My sweat was burning my eyes. My heart was beating so fast.

His was not beating at all.

Anthony called out, "Ambu bag in place. Pump once . . . pump twice . . ."

"His pupils are dilating! I need blood gasses!"

"He's in V-tach!" Jayla yelled.

"Start two lines: lidocaine drip and normal saline. Push both of them hard!" I yelled at Jayla.

"We're losing him!" Anthony yelled.

My hands were sweaty. *I can't panic but I can't fight.* The heart monitor was humming its swan song. Death was in the room, waiting to collect another soul. I got a glimpse at the patient's face. It was like seeing a ghost from my past. *His features . . .*

He looked like Kyle.

Damn!

"Paddles! Charge for defib at two hundred joules! Everybody clear!" I hit him with the paddles, and his body jerked. "Reset at three hundred joules! Clear!" Once again I hit him.

Anthony yelled, "I'm not getting a rhythm!"

"Same again, three hundred joules! Clear!"

Death was standing next to the bed, still waiting.

"Nothing."

I looked at my patient, then at Jayla and Anthony. Defeat was in their eyes.

"Okay. Atropine, one milligram!"

Jayla grabbed the syringe and handed it to me. I stabbed the needle through his chest plate and injected it directly into his heart. "I'm starting chest compressions again."

Over and over again, I pushed on his chest. I felt a rib break, but I couldn't stop. He was going to die, but I couldn't stop. I worked on him for about twenty-five minutes before Dr. DeJesus came.

"Three, one thousand, four, one thousand, five, one thousand . . ."

Dr. DeJesus put her hand on my shoulder. "It's okay. You can stop now, Dr. Scott. Call it."

I exhaled. "Time of death: two fifty-three p.m."

I pulled my gloves off. Jayla and Anthony stood there quietly, staring at me. I looked at Dr. DeJesus, then again at my patient, and I walked out. I felt numb. I replayed everything in my head, trying to think of what else I could have done. Nothing came to mind.

I took a deep breath and walked out of the ER to the doctors' locker room. A few minutes later, Dr. DeJesus came inside and sat next to me.

"Nia, there's nothing more you could have done for him. He was gone before he got here."

"Yeah, I know."

"You did your best. Now you've just got to put it behind you."

I nodded. "Yeah, I know."

Once my shift was over, I quickly gathered my things and left. My mind was on autopilot as I made my way home. That patient's resemblance to Kyle brought back all kinds of feelings I thought I had put behind me. When I got home, I was alone. I broke down and cried. Tears of anguish poured down my face. All I could think of was Kyle.

Hours later, Brandon came home and saw me sitting in bed with a box of tissues half empty. The room was dark with the blinds closed. My face was damp from tears.

"Hey, what's wrong, baby?"

"I had a bad day."

"What happened?"

"I had a bad day."

"Oh, I see."

Tears began to rim my eyes. "I've lost patients before, but this one . . . this got me."

"You're human, and we all have moments when we're vulnerable. But you also got me, and whenever you need support, I got you."

He held me tight in his arms and let me feel whatever I felt. Brandon reminded me that whatever happened in my life, I didn't have to deal with it alone.

Chapter Twenty-six

Insecure

Sabina Singh

There was nothing less attractive than an insecure man. Those were the types of men who were usually the control freaks. I came from a culture where women were submissive to their husbands. My father was a very strict traditional Punjabi man. As a teenager, I couldn't even Google the word "sex." My only clue about sex came from the Bollywood films, where sexual energy was exuding from the screen. Social media was damn near nonexistent for me until I was 17. By that time, my mom and dad were going through their divorce, and I had more freedom. If my father had his way, I would've been in an arranged marriage where, somehow, I was supposed to be this perfect virgin wife who would magically know how to please my husband's sexual needs. That was like asking somebody to cook a three-course meal who'd never been in a kitchen.

But not me. I made it my mission to experience as much sex as I could when I went away to college. I did everything my father forbade me to do. I hated his rules and would never allow myself to be in a relationship with that type of man. The type of man who had you on a dress code and didn't allow you to wear shorts, skirts, or anything tight. No blouse that would show too much skin, or God forbid, anything off the shoulder. The type of man who told you you're not allowed to talk to any other guys, like you were 3 years old or something. Or the type who told you you were not allowed to go to certain places without him.

The funny thing is you can tell which women are with men like that when you see them. The type of girl who's always talkative and outgoing then gets quieter than a church mouse when her man comes around. The type of woman who has to ask for permission to go out somewhere with her girlfriends. Or the girlfriend you've been cool with since elementary school who, all of sudden when she gets with a new guy, is not allowed to hang out with you anymore.

It's a sad thing to see happening to a woman. It's even sadder when it starts happening to you. The funny thing is, or should I say the sad part about it is, you don't even realize it's happening. Little by little a man will tell you small things he wants you to do or not do. At first, you don't trip off of it because they're so minor. The minor things start building into changes, and then the more you begin to give in, you start to become his puppet. I swear, some men are like drugs, and like drugs they should come with a warning label on the side of their ass, listing their side effects, like: warning: this male has been hurt in the past and may be a control freak and insecure. Any future girlfriend may want to avoid dating this male because he may go upside your cranium if enraged.

If only life were so easy, I may not have ended up dating this psycho, Jon. Sure, they don't let all their crazy tendencies out right away. They trap you. And that was exactly what Jon tried to do to me.

Let me start at the beginning.

One morning, I went to Bank of America to open a new account. I signed the waiting sheet to speak with a new account manager and sat down. I had on a white skintight dress and high heels. There were three people already sitting who were ahead of me, but a very attractive man got up from his desk and walked over to the waiting area. He glanced at the sign-in sheet, then glanced at me. We made eye contact and gazed at each other for about five seconds, and then he looked at the sheet again.

"Sabina Singh?"

I smiled. "Yes, that's me."

He returned my smile and extended his hand. "Hi, my name is Jon. Come with me please."

I could tell the other people waiting were pissed off that I was being helped after only being there for all of two minutes. This joker skipped everybody to get to me. I sat at his desk and told him I only wanted to open a simple checking and savings account, and he took care of it. The whole time I could tell he was checking me out.

As he typed on the keyboard, he asked, "Are you married?"

"Excuse me?"

"I mean, is this going to be a joint account with somebody?"

"Ah, no, just me."

He nodded and continued typing. "Okay, well, if your boyfriend wants to be added to the account, we can do that, too."

I grinned. "Ah, I don't have a boyfriend."

"Really? Wow. I'm sorry. I just assumed an attractive woman like yourself would have somebody."

I blushed. "No, just me, myself, and I."

"That's a shame."

He was really flirting with me. I was single at the time and hadn't been dating anybody for a while because I was tired of dating the same wannabe thugs and men who were hustling on the side. I'd dated white men before but nothing serious. Maybe this would be something new.

"Jon, why did you skip all those other people in the lobby?"

He smirked. "How else was I going to get you at my desk?"

"Why would you want to get me at your desk?" I leaned back and waited for his answer.

"So I could find out if a guy like me had a chance to talk to you."

"Well, I think you do."

"Can I have your number so I can talk to you more?"

I smiled and wrote my number on a Post-it Note. How was I supposed to know I was hooking up with Ike Turner?

Well, a day went by, and Jon called me. We talked on the phone, and he was so smooth with it. He told me how he was looking for a good woman and that he hadn't dated anybody in a while because he was looking for the right type of woman. How when he saw me he knew I was different. You know, the typical shit men say when they're trying to get close to you. I was feeling the same kind of way. I'd had my share of losers in the past. At that point, my biggest mistake was hooking up with Tony back in college.

I was young and dumb and having way too much sex. I was doing way too much back then. I was going through a phase back then and thought I was grown. Coming from a sheltered home, I couldn't do anything a normal teenage girl could do. Dating was out of the question, even though I had lost my virginity junior year of high school to a boy named Devon. I would sneak out of the house, and we'd do it in the back seat of his Chevy Impala. I knew my father would have killed me if he found out, but I didn't care. I was horny.

Even so, Devon wasn't that experienced himself, so it wasn't exactly great sex. I didn't know what good sex was back then, but being with him turned me on to Black men. Even if I wanted to date Devon, there was no way my father was going to allow me to date outside of my race. In Punjabi culture, it is frowned upon to be with anybody not Punjabi. Dating in general is frowned upon, and my father loved tradition, but I was anything but that.

By the time I was living in Atlanta, I had my choice of men who wanted me. I had no idea a little Punjabi girl from Chicago would be the most sought-after thing on campus. I was living in Nia's apartment at the time. God, I was so inconsiderate back then. I really regretted that, but at the time Tony was blowing my back out and I was living my best life, or so I thought.

Then things got bad when he introduced me to XTC. He said it would make our sex ten times better. He was right. It was so much more intense, but then sometimes I would black out and not remember what happened the night before. Sometimes I would wake up butt naked in the middle of the floor, not remembering how I got there. Then that one night we had sex in Nia's bed, Nia walked in on us, and I was high as hell. I thought she was going to kick my ass that night. Maybe she should have. It would have knocked some sense into me. When she kicked me out, I moved in with Tony. We were doing X and drinking all the time. I even dropped out of school for a while.

I'd made some bad choices in men, and little did I know, I was about to do that again. Jon wasn't like anybody I'd dated before, so I just knew he would be different. He was sexy, tall, white, and handsome. And it wasn't too long before we were seeing each other on a regular basis. After a few weeks of us going out, I decided to sleep with him, and looking back on it, I should have waited.

Not that the sex was bad. He was good. We went back to my place after dinner, and I invited him in. We sat on the couch and talked about whatever to kill the time, and soon enough we started kissing. Shortly thereafter, we were naked. Jon was a well-endowed man. Not as big as Tony, but big enough. We were lying on my couch doing the whole foreplay thing. We had sex that night, and we continued to see each other.

We were officially dating, and he was really good to me at first, or maybe that was his representative. The first real sign of his controlling nature came one night when we were going out to dinner. I put on the same white dress I had on the day we met.

"Why are you wearing that dress?"

"I like it, and it looks good on me."

"Don't you think it's kinda tight?"

"That's kinda the point. It really shows off my curves."

"I don't see why you have to wear that. It makes you look like you're easy or something."

"So when you first met me in this dress, you thought I was easy?"

"No." He sighed. "I just don't want other guys staring at you like that. You're with me, and I just want your body to be my eye candy, not everybody else's."

I should have known what was up, but I wanted to make him happy, so I changed. Every time we went out from then on, I always asked if he liked what I had on. Clothes that I loved wearing I didn't wear because I wanted Jon to feel comfortable. Never mind how I felt.

The second sign came one day when I was leaving work and Jon was picking me up. I walked out of the building with this guy named Eric. Jon saw us talking, and he thought he was trying to holla. When I got in the car, it was on.

"Who was that?"

"Who was what?"

"That guy you were just talking to!"

I stared at him quizzically. "Him? Oh, that's my co-worker."

He frowned. "Why is he talking to you?"

"Because we're friends and we work together. Why are you tripping?"

"I don't like the way he was looking at you."

"Looking at me like what?" I chuckled. "You don't trust me?"

"I do trust you. I just don't trust him."

I rolled my eyes. "All righty then."

"Promise me you're not going to talk to other guys."

"What? Ever? Jon, I'm not trying to get with nobody else. I'm with you."

He glared at me. "I don't want you talking to him."

"Are you kidding me? Half the damn planet is filled with men! I got no choice but to talk to men."

"You know what I mean! Don't talk to him!"

We argued in the car for a half hour before we pulled off. I couldn't understand why he was bugging. Another insecurity. A few days went by, and we were still kinda funky with each other. By this time, he had moved in with me since I had the bigger apartment. Another mistake. When you're just dating you don't really get to know that person because they put on that mask and only show you the side they want you to see. But when you live together, the mask comes off and the real side comes out. I think I just wanted to make this relationship work because I didn't want to be alone.

When I came home from work, Jon had made a romantic dinner for us. He was a perfect gentleman, and we talked about what happened. Jon explained that he was married before for a few months. His wife cheated on him with a coworker and left him. That was the reason he was so protective of me. I felt sorry for him.

After dinner, Jon put some slow jams on, and we danced in our bedroom. He kissed my neck and slowly pulled off my shirt. Next, he unbuttoned my jeans and slid his hands under my panties. Jon undressed me, and we had sex. The one thing he knew how to do really good was fuck. We were still using condoms. That was something I wouldn't compromise on. Good thing, because our bodies were in sync last night. It was so intense, and we both got ours at the same time.

The next morning Jon woke up and went to work. I was off from work and slept in. When I finally got up, the room was a mess, and I started to clean up. I looked under the bed and saw the condom Jon used last night. I picked it up and looked at it, and my heart immediately began to race. There was no semen in it. I thought back to last night and how intense the sex was. I remembered us cumming together and how amazing it felt. No wonder it did. His ass pulled off the condom, and he came in me. *Bastard!*

I got dressed and ran to the Walgreens down the street, got a Plan B, and took it. *What the hell?* He wasn't a hustler on the streets trappin', but he was doing another kind of trappin' for real! As soon as Jon got home, I went off.

"Are you trying to get me pregnant?"

He tried to look confused at me. "What? What are you talking about?"

"You took the condom off last night!" I showed him the evidence.

"Why would I do that?"

"I don't know! You tell me. You know I don't want to have a baby! You're trying to trap me?"

"Listen, it came off, okay? We didn't have another one here, and I was caught up in the moment. I'm sorry."

"You're sorry? Jon, I could be pregnant!"

"If you were, would that be a bad thing? I'll take care of my responsibilities."

I frowned. "Oh, that's nice to know, but that's not the point! You took advantage of me!"

"Sabina, I'm sorry. I made a mistake and I'm sorry! I love you. Please forgive me, baby. I can't live without you."

I should have kicked his ass out right then, but I was an idiot. We talked about it all night long, and he finally wore me down, and I forgave him. I decided to trust that he wouldn't do that again. I needed to trust that he would never do that again. I wasn't ready to be anybody's mother. I was so tired of being alone and wanted to be loved.

From then on, Jon tried his best to be good to me, and I thought this was some of the things couples go through. *Yeah, right. I bet Nia and Brandon don't have any problems.*

Despite what I said about Jon, I wanted this relationship to work out. He really did have some good qualities. He just needed a good woman by his side. A lot of us complain that we can't find a good man, but we pass up any man who doesn't fit perfectly into what we think they should be. I wanted to give Jon a chance. He deserved it.

Like I said before, it's a sad thing when you start to become "that woman" and don't even realize it. Because once it starts to happen to you and you realize it, it's already too late. Pretty soon, you're sitting in the kitchen with a black eye, wondering how the hell this happened. But I'm getting ahead of myself. I was not that woman. It could never happen to me. I was too smart for that shit. That was what I kept telling myself as I put ice on my face.

Chapter Twenty-seven

Cover Up

Nia Scott

Going back to work the next day was difficult. I still felt a sense of loss that I couldn't quite shake. When I went inside the ER, I saw the look on Anthony's face. He was smiling at me like I did something outstanding. He walked toward me. "Dr. Scott, you were incredible to watch yesterday."

"What do you mean? My patient died."

"I know, but you did everything above and beyond to try to save him. I've never seen anybody work so hard to save a life."

I nodded and walked away. That was unexpected, especially coming from Anthony. As I went toward the doctors' lounge, I spotted Dr. Haugabrook. He was the chief of emergency medicine at Grady. God knows I wasn't in the mood to deal with this short, arrogant ass.

He glared at me. "Dr. Scott, why did you end up killing a patient?"

I craned my neck and matched his glare. "The patient came in with considerable internal injuries."

"Did you tell the patient's father that? Because he was in the waiting room, and he was told his son was in stable condition. Next thing he finds out is that his son died."

"I didn't know that."

He glared at me like he wanted to call me a liar.

"Dr. Haugabrook, it was a trauma stat. I did everything I could to save his life. His injuries were just too extensive."

"Well, his family is asking a lot of questions about what happened, and they are threatening to sue. We will be investigating this further."

He wasn't trying to listen to anything I had to say, but there was no way I was going to let him continue to belittle me as if I did anything wrong.

"Go ahead and investigate. I did everything I could. May I remind you we were in the middle of a snowstorm, and I have no idea how long it took for the paramedics to get to him. Retrace all steps before accusing me of anything. I did everything by the book. No other doctor here could have done more than I did to save him."

He rolled his eyes. "We will see about that."

Whatever! I took ownership of the situation and was unflinching in my stance because I knew I did nothing wrong. He marched away, and I couldn't help but wonder if he would have come down on a male attending the way he did me. I'd dealt with certain men who were biased toward women. They would go out of their way to humiliate us simply to exert their power, but I don't back down to no one.

A week later, Sabina met me for lunch at Chipotle on Ponce De Leon. I got a steak burrito bowl, and Sabina got a chicken burrito bowl.

She took a bite of her food. "What's going on with you?"

I exhaled. "I had a bad shift the other day."

"What happened?"

"A patient died on me, and he reminded me of Kyle."

"Oh, man. I'm sorry, Nia."

"It's all right. I'm fine now." I stared at her. "Sabina, why are you wearing shades? You some type of celebrity now or something? Girl, take them damn things off."

"Girl," she nervously laughed, "I forgot I still had them on." She removed them, and instantly I frowned. Her makeup was caked on like icing on a lopsided cake. She was a natural beauty and never wore a lot of makeup, so it was obvious to me what she was trying to conceal.

"What the hell is that?"

Another nervous laugh. "Girl, you going to think I'm stupid, but it was dark, and I walked right into a door the other night."

"You walked into a door? I know you don't expect me to believe that bullshit."

She shook her head. "You're being dramatic."

"Sabina, did Jon hit you?"

"Jon? Girl, don't be silly! He would never put his hands on me! I bumped into a door. I'm not letting any man hit me!"

"So you bumped into a damn doorknob shaped like a fist? Sabina, did he hit you?"

"Nia, if Jon had hit me, we would still be fighting. And I would leave that fool."

I exhaled. "Seriously, you can tell me the truth. Please."

She forced a smile. "There's nothing to tell."

I really wanted to believe her, but I'd seen it happen too many times in the past to other women I thought would never let themselves be abused by a man. If Sabina didn't want to admit to it happening, I couldn't force her.

"All right, but if you want to talk about it, I'm here."

"I know, but you're blowing this way out of proportion."

"Okay."

The elephant in the room made the remainder of our lunch awkward. Jon didn't seem like the type, but that's how it always is. The way she was covering for this son of a bitch was so obvious. I wanted to help her, but if she wouldn't let me, then what could I do?

When I got home, Brandon was in the bathroom fixing tiles on the wall. Buying this house together was a big step. It actually presented itself at the right time, and we jumped on it. My mom was happy but concerned that we made such a permanent decision before getting married. Although we'd discussed marriage, it had never been a priority for us, but I knew it was coming.

"Hey, baby, what's up?" Brandon got down off the step ladder and pursed his lips for a kiss.

"Nothing much." I kissed him. "Well, maybe something."

"What's wrong?" He looked at me.

"I just had lunch with Sabina, and she showed up with these big shades on."

"Okay . . . and?"

"Well, when she took them off, she had a black eye."

"What? Damn."

"Yeah, she told me she bumped into a door."

"What are we going to do about it?"

"I don't know. Sabina is covering up for him, so nothing can be done until she actually says something."

"How long do you think this has been going on?"

"I'm not sure."

"You think she's scared to leave him?"

"Maybe." I shrugged. "I don't see why she would stay with him if she isn't."

"Do you think I should go talk to her?"

"No. This guy might be the jealous type. I don't want to put her in a worse situation than she is in. I'll go check on her tomorrow."

I went over to Sabina's the next day to see how she was doing and hopefully talk some sense into her. She had become a mature woman and a real friend to me after Kyle's death, and I'd be damned if I let some guy beat on her. I knocked on the door, and a few seconds later she cracked it open.

"Hey, girl, what's up?"

She looked depressed. "Nothing. Why didn't you call first before you came over?"

I stared into her eyes. "Since when do I call before I come?"

She didn't respond. I also noticed she hadn't invited me in yet.

"Are you just going to leave me out here?"

"No." She exhaled and let me in.

I walked inside and saw Jon sitting on the couch watching TV. "Hey, Jon, what's up?"

"Hey, there." He grinned. "Excuse the mess. It's been crazy around here."

It looked like *WWE SmackDown! vs. Raw* in her place. The look on Sabina's face indicated it was that and more.

"Oh, okay."

"I always gotta tell her not to be such a pig, ya know what I mean?" he joked, but nobody laughed. "She needs to stop being so lazy and pick up after herself."

The tension in the air was palpable, and it was obvious that I walked in on the aftermath of some foul shit he had done. Sabina may have been a lot of things, but messy was not one of them. I could see a bruise on her arm that she was doing a bad job at covering up. I felt my heart racing and wanted to kill his ass.

"I'll clean up later."

"I just came by to see what you were doing on Saturday. Brandon and I are going to watch Sean play against the Hawks. He said he can get as many tickets as we need. You two want to come?"

Sabina turned and looked at Jon as if asking for permission. I could tell by his evil deadpan expression he was daring her to say yes. She looked back at me. "We might have plans, but I'll call you if anything changes." Jon got up off the couch, walked up to Sabina, and palmed her ass. "I might have her hemmed in in the bedroom all weekend," he joked, and once again nobody laughed.

I bet you would have her hemmed in by her neck. I wanted to crack his head wide open, but Sabina gave me an uncomfortable smile like she was telling me to please not set him off. Jon walked toward the kitchen.

"Sabina, seriously," I whispered. "We can leave together right now."

She shook her head. "Nia, everything is fine. Okay?" Sabina tried to sound convincing. Not for my sake, but for his. I noticed more bruises on her arm, and she saw me looking at them, then pulled her sleeves down.

"Damn, Sabina!" Jon bellowed. "Why the fuck are there plates in the sink? You can't clean up?"

"Nia, I'll call you later, all right?"

I hugged her and left the apartment with fear in my stomach for her safety. *What should I do?*

Chapter Twenty-eight

Home Cumming

Nia Scott

The Hornets were playing the Hawks in town on Saturday. Sean arrived last night and was staying with us. He was a bit of an NBA star, but thankfully it hadn't gone to his head. He was a starting guard for the Hornets and tended to draw comparisons to another NBA all-star who came out of North Carolina thirty-some years ago. Brandon and Sean were catching up with each other in the living room.

"Yo, that dunk you did the other night was sick."

Sean smiled. "Yeah, they were playing that clip on *SportsCenter* for a minute."

"You know a lot of people are looking at you now. You going to stay or go into free agency?"

"I don't know. I might go into free agency. Depends on who's offering the best deal."

I added my two cents. "Go for the money."

"And we're not even talking about any endorsement deals."

"That's what I'm talking about."

"I'm going to take my time and make my decision."

Sean would make the right choice. I may have gotten on him for his lack of discretion when it came to the women he dealt with, but with his career, he'd made all the correct moves.

"That's wus up. But you know the weather in L.A. is great all year round. Just saying!"

"True, true. Yo, I'm gonna hit the bed. I got to be at the Civic Center at seven in the morning for practice."

"Make sure you practice your fadeaway. You're getting kinda sloppy," I teased.

He laughed and headed to his room. "All right, Coach. Yo, Brandon, you going to be able to drop me off in the morning?"

"I got ya."

I was glad Brandon and Sean were close. He was like an older brother to him.

Life as an ER attending was never dull, but one thing was for sure—the most trying patients always came back, not because they wanted help, but they were destined to make your life miserable. Hence, welcome back, our 74-year-old bigot.

"Oh, great," Anthony sighed, looking at the board. "It's Mr. Grey again."

Jayla shook her head. "I thought he was one of your peoples."

"I was until he saw my Star of David necklace and realized I was Jewish. Old geezer called me every name in the book."

"Well, it's nice to know he's an all-around racist," Jayla told him. "Tell you what . . . I'll take him off your hands."

Anthony looked at her strangely. "Um . . . you do know he hates Black people too?"

She glanced at me. "Of course I do, but today is not the day for his shenanigans. Does he need his shot of cortisone?"

"Probably."

Jayla nodded. "I got him."

"Well, he's all yours. Enjoy."

Anthony quickly walked away. I followed Jayla as she walked into the room. Mr. Grey's face contoured in a scowl when he saw us. I didn't know what was giving him more pain: his shoulder or seeing us.

"What are you colored girls doing in here?"

Jayla remained professional. "I'll be your doctor today, Mr. Grey."

"I don't want any niglets touching me!" He grimaced in pain. "Ow!"

"A niglet?" She turned and looked at me, and I shook my head. That was a new one to me too. "What brings you in today?"

"Whad'da ya think? I'm in pain! Where's my doctor?"

She exhaled. "Dr. Claremont isn't in, so I'm going to have the nurse give you your shot."

"The hell you are, nigger! Aarragh! I can request another doctor, and not that Jew boy either!"

I decided to step in and address him. "That's true, Mr. Grey, you can request another doctor. However, if you insist on Dr. Claremont treating you, you will have to wait until the morning, when he comes in again." I looked at Jayla. "We can get his discharge papers ready."

"What! What about a nurse?"

"Sure," Jayla answered. "That's what I first suggested. Oh, she's Black too."

Mr. Grey's eyes bucked.

"Then there's Nurse Ming Li."

He glared at us. "You two are enjoying this, aren't ya? You're enjoying watching me suffer!"

"No, we're not," Jayla spoke up. "I actually feel sorry for you. I don't get any pleasure watching any human being suffer, but if you want to be seen here, you have to see who's available. If you don't want to do that, you're refusing medical care, and we can send you home and use this bed for a patient who wants our help. The choice is yours. Are we seeing you, or should we get your discharge papers ready?"

He looked at me, then back to Jayla. He looked defeated and nodded. Jayla stepped out of the room and returned a few moments later with Nurse Ming Li, who quickly swabbed his shoulder and gave him the cortisone shot he'd been crying for. Pretty soon the steroid made its way into his system and eased his pain.

We walked away, and I looked at Jayla. "You handled that situation perfectly."

"Thank you. It took everything in me not to—forgive me, Lord—put a pillow over his face."

"Believe me, under different circumstances, I might be the one holding him down for you."

We laughed at our dark humor.

It was game day, and the Hornets were blowing out the Hawks as Sean led the way with forty-six points, ten rebounds, and twelve assists. His seventh triple double this season.

Sabina didn't make it to the game. Jon probably didn't want her hanging out with Brandon and, let alone, my brother. Since I saw her last, I'd tried reaching out to her, but every time I called, she couldn't talk long. It was like he was standing over her shoulder or something. I was really worried about her, but she wouldn't let me help her. I had to find a way to get through to her.

After the game, Sean went out with his teammates to celebrate, and Brandon and I went to City Winery in Ponce City Market for drinks. I was off work the next day, so I was indulging myself with glasses of sweet wine.

Brandon knew what a horny lush I was after a few glasses, and he was grinning like the Cheshire cat. "I can't remember the last time I drank so much." He smirked. "I do. New Year's Eve." "I'm still trying to forget seeing my parents that night." I shuddered at the memory. "Well, at least they're happy together now." "I guess," I said half-heartedly. "I just wish they had had this reconciliation a few years ago." "Sometimes things happen when they should. Not before or not when we want them to." He did have a point. Even within our relationship I couldn't deny that, for better or worse, things happened the way they did for a reason. After a few more drinks, I reached that happy place where I was too drunk to drive but horny enough to have wild sex, so we left.

I pawed at Brandon while we made our way to the front door. He unlocked it. I couldn't wait to feel him inside me.

"Oh, for fuck's sake!" I yelled, annoyed as hell.

Sean was sitting on the couch with his head tilted back, getting some head from some big-booty girl. They must've been wasted as hell because they didn't even hear us come in.

"Oh, snap!"

Sean quickly tapped the girl on her head. She jumped up and wiped her mouth while Sean swiftly pulled his pants up. The goofy grin on his face annoyed me even more.

"Hey, Nia, didn't expect you to get home so early."

"No, really! Dammit, that's my new couch! Why is she sucking your dick on my couch? You have a room!"

"I'm so sorry," she apologized.

Brandon was dying with laughter, and Sean started laughing too.

I glared at them both. "I don't see anything funny about this shit!"

Brandon pulled me closer to him. "Yo, Sean, why don't you take your guest to your room?"

"His room? Oh, you mean where his nasty ass should've been in the first place!"

Sean nodded and took Ms. New Booty's hand and got up. "Good looking out, dawg." As they strolled by us, Sean gave Brandon some dap. The nerve of these two acting like this was a frat house!

"What the hell was that?"

"Calm down. You think he hasn't had his dome shined before?"

"Of course he has! But I'm tired of seeing my family members getting nasty!"

"Okay, okay, just follow me." He took my hand.

"Where are we going?"

"Would you rather stand there and be mad or watch me do something nasty to you?"

I grinned and instantly calmed down. "Nasty, you say?"

"Let's show them how we get down in the A."

I smiled and followed Brandon into our bedroom. I quickly forgot about my brother and his shenanigans and got into some of my own.

Chapter Twenty-nine

Valentine's Day Massacre

Nia Scott

Sean left yesterday with his team back to the West Coast. As much as I loved him, if he brought one more freak up in my house, I would have choked him out. I was on my lunch break trying to enjoy a Caesar salad but not having much success. My mind was on Sabina, so I decided to call her, and to my surprise she answered.

"Hey, Sabina what's up?"

Her voice was low. "Nothing much."

"We haven't talked in a minute. You okay?"

"Sorry. I've been kinda busy."

"Are you at work?"

"No. I . . . decided to stay home today. I feel a little sick."

I frowned. "Are you okay? Seriously, are you hurt?"

"I'm fine," she replied softly.

I didn't believe her. "Sabina, you can leave him and come stay with us."

"I'm fine, Nia. Jon just lost his temper, and we had a little fight."

"Sabina, he has no right to put his hands on you at all! You don't have to stay there with him. It's your apartment. We can go to the police station, file a report, and get a restraining order."

She didn't respond.

"Sabina, you have got to get out of there. Listen, I'll—"

"Nia, I gotta go. I'll talk to you later."

"Sabina!"

The line went dead. Jon must have been in the other room or something. *This is crazy. I have to get her away from him before he kills her.*

After our first few years together, Valentine's Day became kinda dumb. Brandon and I celebrated our love every day of the year. We both came to the conclusion that it was a corporate holiday designed to boost sales in candy and flowers. The Hallmark company was the real Illuminati here.

My shift at the hospital went by slower than most, with patients crankier than usual. On top of it, I had to work with Dr. Haugabrook, who told me he was going to see more patients than me. *When did patient care become a race?* I would have rather seen the bigot. I couldn't wait to get home, take a hot shower, and fall asleep in Brandon's arms.

Thoughts of Sabina overcame me on my drive home. I wanted to call her but was unsure if I should. Brandon's car was in the driveway when I arrived home, and immediately, a sense of calmness rushed over me. As soon as I walked through the front door, I saw a trail of rose petals on the floor leading upstairs. A grin spread across my face.

I put down my bag and followed the trail, which led me to the bathroom where Brandon was standing with roses in his hands. White and red candles were lit all around the edge of the garden tub. A hot bubble bath was behind him, and the scent of sweet cherries wafted through the air.

"This is so nice."

"Just a little something for you."

Brandon kissed my lips and handed me the roses. I inhaled the beautiful scent. "I need to put these in some water."

"I got that." He took them from me. "You just make yourself comfortable in the tub."

"As you wish."

Brandon walked out of the bathroom, and I undressed. My mind was still on Sabina, but I was going to make the best of this night. Slowly, I stepped into the warm water, and I sank into the foaming bubbles. My body needed pampering like this after the last few days I'd had. I closed my eyes, leaned my head back, and let Calgon take me away.

"How does that feel?"

I opened my eyes and saw Brandon dressed in his robe, holding a bottle of Moscato and two wineglasses.

I smiled. "Simply fabulous."

Brandon placed the wineglasses on the edge of the tub and filled them. Then he took off his robe. No matter how many times I saw him naked, he always managed to turn me on. His muscular arms, chest, and abs seemed to glisten in the steam-filled room. My eyes traveled down to his large chocolate manhood. That mushroom-tipped pole dangled so seductively between his muscular thighs. He got in the tub behind me, opened his legs, and I slid back and rested against his chest, feeling his half-hard penis against my ass.

"This is exactly what I needed." I closed my eyes and took it all in.

"It's all for you."

"What would I do without you in my life?"

"I was just thinking the same thing."

"After all the things we been through. All the drama, all the mood swings. I don't think any other man would have stuck with me for this long."

"Nia, you're are the strongest woman I've ever known. Most men search a lifetime for a lady like you. Then when they do get someone like you, they don't know how to appreciate her. Not me though."

"You always treat me like a queen even when I act like a royal bitch."

He laughed. "Nah, you're never that."

"Yeah, right."

"But you know something, after all these years of us being together, I'm ready to do something new."

"What do you mean?"

"I mean us just being together isn't enough anymore."

I opened my eyes. "What are you saying?"

Brandon handed me a glass of Moscato. "Look how sparkly your wine is."

I looked at the glass and saw a gold ring with a huge diamond stone set in the middle.

"Oh, my God, Brandon!"

"I'm tired of being just your man. I want to be your husband. I want you to be my wife. Will you please marry me, Nia Scott?"

I turned and faced him. I never thought I would feel this way. Although Brandon and I had talked about marriage, it always seemed far away. Now it all just felt surreal, like, *is this really happening now?* Brandon was the perfect man for me. If Kyle asked me, I would've thought of a million reasons why I should have said no. But with Brandon, all I could say was . . .

"Yes."

He smiled. "Really?"

"Yes, I will."

I repeated it joyfully, then took the ring out of the glass and gave it to him. He slid it on my finger. We kissed each other passionately like it was the first time. I couldn't believe how happy I was. Brandon took me out of the tub and carried me to our bed. All I wore was my engagement ring. We were still soaking wet, but we didn't care. I wanted him as much as he wanted me. Soon we were making love, and I felt overcome with pleasure and joy. I felt him not just deep between my legs, but in my heart. We rolled from side to side, giving ourselves to each other both physically and mentally.

"I love you, babe."

"I love you too."

We made love until we both exploded with ecstasy and collapsed in each other's arms, totally spent. I never thought I would be this happy about getting married. That was always my mother's dream, but now it was mine because I was finally ready.

We both fell asleep after hours of lovemaking, but our joyful night was soon cut short. My cell phone rang in the middle of the night. I reached over for it and answered.

"Hello? Yes, this is."

Brandon raised his head and looked at me. "Who is it?"

"What happened? Oh, my God. We'll be right there."

I hung up the phone.

"Babe, what's wrong?"

"It was the hospital. Sabina's been brought in. It's pretty bad."

Chapter Thirty

Survivor

Nia Scott

When we arrived at the hospital, Sabina was still unconscious and in the ICU. I was glad she had me listed as an emergency contact. Sabina's next-door neighbor called the police after they heard shouting and a girl screaming for help.

When I saw her lying there swollen, bruised, and lifeless, all I could do was cry. I held her hand and beat myself up on the inside because I knew I should have tried harder to get through to her and make her leave.

Brandon walked back in the room and stood next to me. "Well, Dr. Morgan said she may drift in and out of consciousness for a while, but her injuries aren't life-threatening."

That was a relief to my ears.

"I know you're blaming yourself for this, but there was nothing more you could have done."

"I'm tired of hearing that. Every time something bad happens to someone close to me, it's always, 'There's nothing more you could have done.' When am I going to be able to do something to help somebody?" This was more of a rhetorical question I didn't expect Brandon to have an answer for. "I'm sorry." I looked at him. "I didn't mean to direct that at you."

He rubbed my shoulders. "It's okay. I understood what you meant."

"You're way too good to me."

"I wanted today to be a perfect day for you. I'm sorry this happened."

"It was perfect, baby." I looked at the ring on my finger. "There's no way either of us could have known this would happen today."

"Well, it looks like you did get through to her."

"What do you mean?"

"I talked to Atlanta PD, who followed Sabina here. They said there were a couple of suitcases by the door. She just didn't get out in time."

I frowned as tears rolled down my cheeks. "That sorry muthafucker. I can't believe he did this to her."

"Since he fled the scene, there's a warrant out for his arrest for aggravated battery. It's just a matter of time before they find him, baby."

"When she comes out of this, I want her to stay with us."

"I was thinking the same thing."

Brandon stayed in the ICU waiting room, while I never left Sabina's side. I drifted off to sleep with my head resting next to hers. A few hours later, I felt somebody stroking my hair, and I looked up and saw Sabina looking at me.

I took her hand. "Thank goodness you're awake."

"Water," Sabina whispered.

I poured out a cup and held the straw steady between her lips. She took a few small sips, grimaced, and looked around the room. "How . . . long?"

"Just a few hours."

Tears rimmed her eyes. "Is he?"

"No, he's gone. He's not going to touch you again."

"I tried to fight him."

I nodded. "I know you did."

More tears rolled from her eyes. I grabbed some tissues and dried her face. I started to cry too.

"I wanted to call you . . . but he wouldn't . . . let me."

"I know you did. I know."

I spent the rest of the night consoling Sabina until she fell asleep again.

Later that day, after I got some sleep at home, I went back to the hospital to see Sabina. She was awake and in her own room on the third floor, out of ICU. She smiled when I entered the room.

"How do you feel?" I sat down beside her.

"Like a damn punching bag. I should've left the very first time he hit me."

"It doesn't matter, Sabina. What matters most is that you're alive."

Her eyes focused on the ring on my finger, and a smile spread across her face. "Brandon finally popped da question?"

I smiled. "Yeah, it still feels surreal. Even though I always knew we would get married at some point, it's the way he did it that still gets me."

"Brandon is a good man, Nia. Trust me. There aren't too many men out there like him."

"I know. When I was younger, I thought getting married would mean giving up my goals and becoming like my mother, but now I see I can do both because Brandon was right by my side the entire time."

She gave me a faint smile. "I'm glad to hear you say that."

I took her hand. "I know there's a good man out there for you, too."

She nodded, but I could tell she didn't believe me. Sabina exhaled and took a moment to gather her thoughts.

"I . . . want to tell you everything."

"You don't have to. It's not necessary."

"No, I need to tell you. I haven't been able to tell anybody else."

"Okay."

Chapter Thirty-one

What's Love Got to Do with It?

Sabina Singh

I didn't know why I was allowing myself to be sucked deeper and deeper into this twisted relationship with Jon. I should've ended it as soon as he started showing me his irrational side, but I didn't. My first mistake. It didn't get real ugly until after the night we went out with Nia and Brandon. After we got home, he was mad for some reason. I walked out of the bedroom and saw him sitting on the couch.

"I had a lot of fun tonight hanging out with them. And the food was good, too."

He didn't respond. I shrugged my shoulders and walked into the kitchen. *"Baby, do you want a drink?"*

"Why didn't you tell me you and Brandon dated?"

"What? We didn't date. When we first met, we went out to a club together as friends. We didn't even kiss."

"What were you doing, just bumping and grinding on each other? Testing the waters?"

"Calm down. Brandon always had a thing for Nia, and I wasn't interested in him after that night."

Jon got up and walked toward me. *"How you going to have me going out all hee-hee, ha-ha with him when you used to be feeling him? Had me sitting there looking like a goddamn idiot!"*

I rolled my eyes. "Why are you blowing this out of proportion? We all have been friends for years. Nobody even cares about that shit anymore."

"So it was all right just to embarrass me like that in front of them?"

"Embarrass you? Oh, please, I'm tired of talking about this shit. It wasn't a big—"

You ever have something happen to you that you knew happened but you couldn't believe it just did? I felt pain across my face. Did he really just hit me? I was just standing there in a daze. Once it dawned on me that I just got pimp slapped, I was ready to get up and get the fuck out of there, but then he started to cry.

"I . . . I'm sorry. I can't believe I did that."

He got on his knees and hugged me, not allowing me to move. He was sobbing like a child. I didn't know if I was still in shock or what. I was trying to process it all, and then I felt sorry for him like a damn fool. I wiped the tears from his eyes.

"I'm sorry, baby. I just get so scared I'm going to lose you. I don't know what I'll do without you."

"It's . . . okay"

"I'm sorry, baby . . . I can't believe I . . . I . . . did that. I'll never ever do that to you again."

"It's going to sound weird to you, Nia, and looking back on it, it doesn't make sense to me either now. But I felt if I left him, I would be running out on him like his ex-wife. We went to the bedroom, and we had makeup sex. I guess at the time it felt like we were making love because my feelings were so intense it was so emotional.

"I fooled myself into thinking that I was in love with him. I knew this wasn't right, but I just chose to believe the lie because it was easier to believe than the truth. Besides, how was I going to face you? I know you might not believe this, Nia, but what you think of me matters a lot. You of all people knew how I was back in the day and how far I've come. The last thing I wanted was to be looked at as a victim.

"When I saw you a few days later, I thought you wouldn't understand, so I kept on making up excuses. I just knew I was in love with Jon, or thought I was, and nobody understood the kind of bond we had. But the truth was it was a toxic trauma bond we shared. But at the time, nothing could change my mind about him. We didn't have another serious fight until one night his friends came by and they were watching the game. Me being the good girlfriend, I tried to be nice to his friends and make conversation with everybody, but that was a big mistake. After they left, all hell broke loose!"

"What do you think you were doing tonight?"

"What do you mean?"

"Don't play dumb with me! What the fuck were you doing flirting with my friends?"

"I wasn't flirting, Jon. I was just making conversation."

He marched toward me.

"Calm down, Jon."

He hemmed me in against the wall by my neck. "Don't tell me what the fuck to do!"

"Stop it! You're hurting me!" I saw the rage in his eyes.

"Shut the fuck up! You don't talk to any man! You hear me?" His hand squeezed my throat.

"Get off me!"

"What?" He backhanded me, and I fell to the floor. "What did I tell you about fucking talking back to me!" He put his foot in my ribs, and all the air left my body.

"Let's just say I learned to keep my mouth closed around any man around me. Once again, he would apologize, and we would have sex, and I guess in his mind that meant all was forgiven. I wanted to tell you what was happening to me, but I was so scared of what he would do to me. He didn't like it when I would talk to you on the phone, so that's why I kept my distance from you. I started staying home from work because I didn't want to make up a dumb excuse why my lip was busted or why my body was sore. I finally got the courage to leave while he was at work. I didn't care about my apartment. I just wanted to get out. This muthafucka must've known I was about to dip, because he came home early. He never came home early."

"Hey, baby, what are you doing home so early?"

"I can't come home now?"

"That's not what I meant. You're home early, that's all."

"Where are you going all dressed up?"

"Nowhere. I'm just chilling."

"Uh-huh, is that right?"

"Do you want me to get you a drink?"

"Yeah, you do that."

I nervously fixed him a drink, and then he walked toward the bedroom. I followed him quickly. After a quick look around, he found my suitcase. We stared at each other for a few seconds before I decided to make a break for it. I threw the drink at him and ran toward the door. Jon grabbed me by my hair as I opened it.

"You trying to leave me, bitch?"

"Get off me!"

He pulled me by the hair and threw me on the floor. "Get your ass back in here! I'm going to have to teach your ass a lesson."

"Somebody help me!"

He covered my mouth and placed me in a choke hold like he was in the WWE. Then that sadistic bastard jabbed his finger into my ear. "Shut your mouth!"

I screamed in so much pain and felt blood coming from my ear. I somehow elbowed him in his nuts, and *that forced him to let me go. In that moment, it felt like something in my mind snapped. I hated him with every part of my being. I didn't want to run anymore. I wanted to kill him. "Fuck you!" He charged toward me, and at that point I knew I was in real danger. So I fought him back as hard as I could. I was swinging on him and scratching the shit out of him. He got a grip on my neck, and I looked in his eyes and saw nothing even human anymore. I thought I was going to die. That was my last thought before blacking out.*

Chapter Thirty-two

Roommates Again

Nia Scott

I couldn't stop the tears from falling down my face while Sabina told me what she had been through. I thought I hated Jon's ass more than she did. *Why do I still feel like I should've done more?* Sabina was my friend, and I knew she was in trouble. I couldn't imagine how it must have really felt to have someone you thought you loved beat you. What was scary was the fact that Jon was still out there.

The next day, Sabina was discharged from the hospital, and Brandon and I moved her into our house. The police assured us they would try to find Jon's friends and family, but I didn't know if Sabina knew much to lead them in the right direction. After what happened at her apartment, she was able to break the lease with no problem. During her time in the hospital, Brandon and I moved most of her furniture into storage. I could tell Sabina was a little embarrassed coming to stay with us until Jon's psycho ass was caught, but this was her only alternative. After a couple of days of recuperating, she seemed to be more at ease being at our home. Sabina was ready to go back to work as well. I was glad she was gaining her confidence. Us living together under the same roof again was like déjà vu. Sometimes we'd look at each other and laugh about the past.

"Do you remember that guy you used to talk to? Darius, I think his name was?"

"Yeah, Darius. What about him?"

"Do you know that fool tried to holla at me while you were in the next room?"

Her jaw hit the floor. "What! That's why you were so pissed off around him?"

"Yeah, he was almost as trifling as Tony's ass."

"Oh, man . . . Tony. Nia, I'm really sorry about that night. I know I've apologized a million times about that, but I feel so bad about it."

"Looking back on it now, it's almost comical."

"I just keep on picking the wrong type of man. Why do I do that? I really thought Jon was different, ya know?"

"Don't feel bad. He fooled us all. He didn't look like the type to do that, but there's no one look for deranged."

"For a second, I thought it was me. I keep asking myself, what did I do to trigger him? Then I realized it wasn't me. It's him. No wonder his first wife left his ass."

"Well, you fought like hell, and you survived. That's what matters."

Things at the hospital were going good, even with Dr. Haugabrook taking a more active role in watching me like a hawk, trying to find something to criticize. I could tell he was upset that I was found not negligible in the death of the young man who died from chest injuries.

After running around the ER seeing patients, I was finally able to take a break. I was still surprised to see how many frontline health care professionals smoked like they didn't see all the patients we had with heart disease, lung cancer, emphysema, and chronic bronchitis. *Crazy.*

My mind was on Brandon and our wedding day. We hadn't set a date yet. Hell, we hadn't even told our parents yet. I knew my mom would be bouncing off the walls with joy. She'd probably want to come down to Atlanta and plan the whole damn thing. *Well, maybe I should let her do it. Lord knows I don't know anything about planning a wedding. When the hell are we going to find time to do this?*

The rest of my shift went relatively smoothly after Dr. Haugabrook left for the day. I swore that man could make a nun catch a charge.

Brandon's birthday was coming up, and I needed to go shopping for his gift. I had no idea what I was going to get him. *Maybe I could just go to Victoria's Secret and buy something revealing. That would be more of a gift for myself. Nah, he likes me naked anyway. Or maybe I should go online and look at some things. The new Galaxy Note is coming out. I know he would love that.*

I took out my keys as I walked to my car in the parking garage. Suddenly, someone grabbed me from behind. Next thing I knew, I was thrown into the door of an SUV parked next to me. I banged my head hard against the door, dazed and confused. My nerves were shot. My heartrate skyrocketed to a frantic pace. I glanced up at my attacker and saw his evil glare looking back at me.

"Fucking bitch," Jon growled.

I yelled while trying to scramble back to my feet. My head was throbbing with pain, and I could feel blood trickling down my brow. I was boxed in between the cars with nowhere to go.

"This is all your fault! You turned her against me!"

"What? You crazy-ass White boy!"

He lunged toward me and grabbed my neck. His grip was strong. His hazel eyes looked dark, like he was looking through me. I felt the back of his hand across my face nearly taking my head off, and then I felt his fist in my ribs knocking the wind out of me. It felt like fire in my side.

"You put all that shit in Sabina's head! She belongs to me!"

I'd never been this scared in my life as I tried to get on my feet. I suddenly knew how Sabina felt. He had a freaking death grip around my neck. My back was pinned up against a car, and I couldn't breathe.

"Where is she?"

He shouldn't have said that. My fear was now replaced with anger. After what he did to Sabina, I'd never let him touch her again.

I managed to get a grip on my keys, and in one fluid motion, I slashed the jagged edge of my door key across his face. His blood skeeted across mine. Jon screamed in pain and let his grip on me go. I started to gasp for air, then gathered enough strength to scream.

"Help me! Someone help me! Help!"

There was nobody in sight. Just me and this maniac.

"Goddamn bitch!"

He punched me across my face, and I fell to the ground. I tried to crawl away from him, but his hands grabbed my left ankle. I turned over and swung my right foot into his face. I smashed my Nikes on his mouth, and blood spurted from his lips.

"Somebody help me!" I screamed again.

Fortunately, there were some guys getting off the elevator who heard me screaming. "Hey. Get away from her!" They ran toward us.

Jon let me go and ran. One of the guys chased after him while the other rushed toward me. "Are you okay?"

"No."

The next few minutes were fuzzy. I was dizzy and could barely think straight. My emotions were all over the place. Jon was legit crazy. A fuckin' coward who preyed on women.

The guy who helped me was a security guard named Alberto. He called the ER, and within minutes, I was being rushed through the trauma entrance upstairs. My colleagues were shocked to see me being brought in on a stretcher.

Alberto took the report of what happened and notified the police so I could file a report later. I was so thankful he came along when he did. Lord knows what could have happened.

I was concerned about Jon's blood on my skin. I had no idea what diseases he could have. Dr. DeJesus was able to examine me.

"Looks like all you need are three stitches for the cut on your head. We also did a rapid STD test, and it was negative. The other results could take about a week or two to come back."

"Great. What about my ribs? Is anything broken? It felt like he rearranged some internal organs."

"You're banged up pretty good, but we were unable to do any X-rays because of your pregnancy."

"Say what now? Pregnant?" I repeated in shock.

She nodded. "Your blood test came back positive. You're pregnant, Nia."

For the next few minutes, I just lay there in a state of shock. A million questions ran through my mind. A million questions I didn't have the answers to. *Do I really want to have a baby now? If I keep it, everything in our lives will change. If I end it now, what will Brandon say? Should I tell him?*

A few minutes later, Brandon showed up with Sabina by his side. Fear and anxiety were on their faces.

He hugged me. "Are you all right?"

"I'll live."

Sabina took my hand. "Nia, I'm so sorry."

I shook my head. "It's not your fault."

"Did the police take a report?"

"Security did and notified them. They're going to call me at home later, but they're sending a patrol car to our house in case he shows up."

Brandon frowned. "He better hope they find him first, because if he comes around, I'm going to kill him."

I caressed his arm. "Brandon, let the police do their job."

"They better."

"I just want to go home."

He nodded.

I didn't want to tell him I was pregnant. Not right there and then. Not in the frame of mind he was in. He would probably go insane with the thought that Jon attacked not only me but also his unborn child. The more I thought about it, having a child terrified me.

Chapter Thirty-three

March Madness

Nia Scott

I told my parents what happened, and my dad wanted me to jump on the first thing smoking back to Chicago. I pleaded with him to make him understand I was okay and I wasn't going to let that psycho run me out of town or from my life. I wished I were as brave as I sounded on the phone. The police still had a patrol car in our neighborhood every night. While I had my parents on the phone, I told them about my engagement, and like I knew, my mom was filled with joy. Brandon still didn't know about the baby. I was still trying to find the right moment to tell him.

After the incident in the parking lot, Brandon became even more protective of me and wanted to go everywhere I went. Even on casual runs to the store or wherever. It had been a few days since the attack, so I understood he still had his guard up. I wanted to run to Cumberland Mall to pick up a few things, and he insisted on coming.

"Brandon, you're going to have to go somewhere when I go in the store," I told him when he parked.

He looked at me matter-of-factly. "I'm not leaving you alone anywhere."

"How am I supposed to buy your birthday gift with you standing over my shoulder?"

"Nia, this fool could be anywhere waiting for you."

"I seriously doubt Jon is stupid enough to attack me in the middle of the mall."

"We didn't think he was going to attack you where you work either, but he did."

"I get it, but, babe, we can't live in fear forever."

"I just don't want to take any chances. I don't know what I'd do if something happened to you."

"Baby, anything can happen at any time."

"I know. That's why I think I'm going to buy a gun."

"What? No, absolutely not."

"Nia."

"Brandon, I am not living in a house with a gun in it. I see patients every day with gunshot wounds. Sometimes with their own gun. I can't."

"I think we need one."

"After what happened to me with Kyle? You expect me to live in a house with a gun?"

"Nia, that was a totally different situation, and you know it."

His comment pissed me off, and I glared at him. "A gun is a gun, period, and I said no."

"Okay," he said, defeated. "No guns."

I got out of the car and marched angrily toward the mall's entrance.

"I'll wait for you right here," Brandon shouted so I could hear him, and he sat on the bench outside.

After I was done shopping, Brandon was where he said he would be. I was still upset and stomped back to the car. We rode back home in silence.

After we got back from shopping, I was still not talking to him. He sat on the couch and watched YouTube stuff he liked while I went in the other room and relaxed with a book. I was going to tell him about the pregnancy when we got home, but I was not in the mood. A few hours passed, and although Brandon tried speaking to me, I didn't have much to say.

"Hey, Nia, can I speak to you for a moment?" Sabina asked when she saw me walk past Brandon without saying a word.

"Sure." I followed her into her bedroom.

"What's going on? Something isn't right. I'm causing issues with you and Brandon, aren't I?"

"Oh, no! Sabina, you're fine." I felt bad that she thought that and didn't realize how my actions were coming off. "We just had a fight in the car."

"Oh, what about?"

I looked at her. "Brandon wants to buy a gun."

"What?"

"I couldn't believe he would even dream about having a gun in here."

"Well, you were attacked, Nia. And although it's not the smartest idea, it may be for the best."

"I know. I just feel like between everything that's happening with me at work, the idea of wedding planning, and now this, my stress level is at an all-time high."

"Is that all? It seems like there's more bothering you."

She's right. This whole pregnancy thing has been killing me inside. I needed to tell somebody.

"There is something else going on. Something big." I exhaled. "Sabina, don't say anything, but the night I was attacked, I found out I was . . . pregnant."

"Oh, my God. Nia, that's wonderful news, isn't it?"

"I don't know if it is. I have my career ahead of me. Do I put that on pause now?"

"You don't have to stop. It'll be an adjustment, but you can still do it. You haven't told Brandon yet, have you?"

"No, and neither will you. I just need to figure out what I'm going to do."

"Nia, c'mon."

"I'm not even sure I want to be anyone's mother." *What kind would I be? Would I end up screwing up a kid's life? I'm not ready for this.*

Since my attack, security was more visible at the hospital. They gave me a week off to recover, and when I returned, even Dr. Haugabrook was semi-nice. In other words, that meant he didn't talk to me. The baby thing was killing me, and I was still giving Brandon the cold shoulder.

The day was going by rather smoothly with no real drama. I got a text message from Brandon that he was in the lobby, and he wanted to know if I could take lunch. I replied that I would meet him in ten minutes and we could go grab something to eat.

We went to a café down the street and had lunch together. It was awkward, to say the least. I wasn't used to us being like this around each other. It was like an 800-pound gorilla in the room.

"Nia, I don't like the tension between us. It's not us."

"I agree."

"I'm just on guard. Every time you walk out the door, I wonder 'what if,' and as a man, that's not a good space to be in."

I nodded. "I shouldn't have gotten so mad about it. I know you were simply trying to protect me, and I appreciate that. It's one of the many things I love about you."

The air between us finally became light.

I looked at Brandon. "I'm sorry."

We kissed each other. This would have been the perfect time to let him know I was pregnant, but I couldn't bring myself to do it.

Chapter Thirty-four

All Falls Down

Nia Scott

The past month and a half were rough. I still hadn't said anything to Brandon about being pregnant. I was glad I confided in Sabina, although she felt I should tell him. I didn't know if I wanted a child now. I'd seen first-hand how things could go wrong in a relationship, and to have the possible responsibility of raising a child on my own, or coparenting, was not something I wanted to do. The situation with crazy-ass Jon on top of it all wasn't helping.

This morning at work was horrible. Morning sickness had me puking in the ladies' room. Nothing stayed down. As I was walking toward a patient's room, something suddenly rushed up my throat, and I ran to the bathroom and threw up in the toilet. It was the most disgusting feeling I'd ever felt. I stayed in the bathroom for another fifteen minutes until my stomach settled down.

Once I got home, I started seriously thinking I needed to see my ob-gyn. I guessed I'd avoided going because I'd been in denial about being pregnant. Also, I wanted to discuss my options, especially at my age. I'd always felt abortions were an easy way out, but now that the shoe was on my foot, my opinion had definitely changed. My mother would kill me if she even thought I was considering getting one. We were supposed to talk later tonight to discuss wedding plans, but I really wasn't in the mood. Brandon walked into our bedroom. I glanced at him, then looked away. He could feel that my energy was off.

"Hey, baby, what's on your mind?"

I forced a smile. "Just thinking about the wedding and how we're going to find time to do it."

"We haven't even set a date for it yet."

"I know. I'm still trying to find the right time."

"Take your time. If you want to go over the calendar together, we can."

"Thanks."

Brandon pulled out his phone and turned on Bob Marley's "I Wanna Love You." I smiled as he held out his hand for me, and I took it.

"The first time you played this, you almost got some."

"I know. Let's hope I do better this time."

We danced to the music, and I rested my head on his chest. I felt so safe in his arms, like nothing could harm me. I wished I could feel this way all the time. *I should tell him. He has a right to know.* Brandon would be so happy to be a father, and he'd be a great one at that. Brandon would never forgive me if I had an abortion. I couldn't hurt him like that.

"Brandon, there's something I have to tell you."

"What is it?"

"I'm . . . pregnant."

His mouth dropped. "You're what?" He beamed with joy. I was still shocked I told him. "You're pregnant? I can't believe it."

He was so happy. I, on the other hand, wasn't. Why couldn't I feel like this? *I can't have a baby now.*

"I'm going to be a father!"

I stood there numb. Brandon looked in my face and noticed my lack of enthusiasm.

"Nia, it's going to be all right. I know this isn't what you planned on, but we can do this together."

I shook my head. "I don't know. I've never had that motherly desire in me."

"I understand. It's a big change for you, and for us, but you know what? We can do anything together. Nia, there is no other woman I would want to have a child with. He or she is going to have the strongest, most loving mother ever."

"Are you sure?"

"No doubt! I'm going to be a father. This is crazy!"

I nodded my head as he touched my stomach. Hearing him say that made me feel so much better. We spent the night cuddling in each other's arms.

My ob-gyn was able to get me in next week. I still wasn't sure if I wanted to have this baby, but I felt better that Brandon knew. I was planning a wedding and having a baby all at the same time. This was bananas. If I told my mom, she'd be on the first plane down here.

Today not even that little troll of a man, Dr. Haugabrook, could even get to me. I had more important shit on my mind.

"Who admitted Ms. Locke to the third floor?" Dr. Haugabrook demanded to know. "I discharged her three hours ago."

I walked up toward him. "I did. Why?"

He sighed. "We do not admit every Tom, Dick, and Harry with the flu. I thought you'd at least know that much."

That remark almost put me over the top. I wanted to cut his throat and watch the life leak out of him. Let him drown in his own blood. It'd be justified homicide. Instead, I smiled through clenched teeth.

"Robert, she came back to the ER. Her temperature was a hundred and three and rising."

"It wasn't that high when I examined her."

"She was under acute respiratory distress and had viral pneumonia. I thought you'd at least know that much considering you examined her. I guess you must have missed it, Robert. It's a good thing she came back and Dr. Spencer did a thorough comprehensive exam."

I stared at him as his usual stupid expression spread across his face. He knew he fucked up. If she had died, it would've been on him. That was the same reason why Black women believed their complaints and symptoms were often dismissed. White doctors had a history of ignoring a Black woman's pain, and they were less frequently referred to specialists.

"Yeah, well, that's good for her."

He walked away quickly. Jayla was standing within earshot of our conversation and walked toward me.

"I don't think Dr. Haugabrook likes being called out on his mistakes."

"That or a future ER attending who just happened to be Black showed him up. Keep up the good work, Dr. Spencer."

She blushed, gave me a smile, and walked off to see to her next patient. Putting Robert in his place made me feel good. That good feeling had me thinking about my talk with Brandon last night. He really made me feel better about everything. As I walked down the hall, I felt nauseated again. *Damn morning sickness.* I started to walk toward the bathroom, and then a sharp pain hit me like someone stabbed me in the stomach with a knife. The pain stopped me in my tracks, and I felt cramping in my abdomen. I grabbed the handrail down the hallway and took another step. Once again, the discomfort cut through me. My vision became blurry, and I felt lightheaded as I fell to my knees in pain.

I heard Dr. Spencer yell my name. "Dr. Scott!"
Something's not right. I felt so much pain.
"Dr. Scott, are you okay?"
"No. Oh God, it hurts so much."
She looked down and saw blood staining my pants.
She yelled, "I need a stretcher! Stat!"

I wasn't sure how much time passed, but I was in a room alone and felt numb. I felt dead inside as if someone had reached inside me, ripped out my organs, then shoved them back in. The meds I was given masked most of the pain, but I knew what happened. My ob-gyn, Dr. Anderson, entered the room.

"Nia, there is no easy way to say this, but it appears that you had a miscarriage," she told me somberly.

I stared at her, unable to find the words for what I was feeling at that moment. She tried her best to console me, but I tuned her out. I thought she said they called Brandon and he was on his way here.

Why do I feel like this? I didn't want this baby anyway. So why did I feel so empty inside? I closed my eyes and tried to comprehend my mixed feelings. *This is what I wanted, right?*

My door opened, and I saw Brandon standing there. The pain on his face hit me like a bus. No words were spoken, but I knew how he felt, and without any warning, I fell apart. Tears streamed uncontrollably. Brandon walked over to me and held me in his arms. I could feel his heart breaking.

I lost the baby. *Did I wish our child away? How could I be this selfish? How could he still love me and want to marry me after what I've done?*

Chapter Thirty-five

A Time to Heal

Nia Scott

It'd been a few weeks since I lost the baby. All I could do was sit at home and daydream about what my baby would have looked like. "My baby." I never referred to it as that until I lost it. Was it a boy or a girl? I'd never know. I felt like because I didn't want it, my body found a way to reject it. Brandon tried his best to be supportive, but I could see in his eyes that he was hurting inside.

I took some time off of work and spent days sitting in front of the TV, zoning out. Sabina came in and knew I was depressed. She tried not to show too much that she was hurt too. Sometimes I forgot that Sabina was dealing with her own situation with Jon. Even though she tried not to show it, at night I could hear her crying in her room. This poor girl had been through so much.

"How you doing?" Sabina asked.

I shrugged. "I'm fine."

"That was a stupid question. I'm sorry."

"It's all right. How was your day?"

"You don't want to hear about that mess."

"Yes, I do. It would take my mind off of things."

Sabina thought about it, then sat next to me on the couch. "Well," she sighed, "this guy named Eric asked me out on a date."

I looked at her. "And?"

"And what?"

"What did you say to him?"

"I said I couldn't."

"Why not?"

"I can't go out with anybody else right now. Crazy-ass Jon might be hiding behind a bush, under a car, or up in a tree."

"Yeah, you got a point. He's crazy enough."

"I don't want to put anybody else in danger because of me."

"I understand."

"Even though I set all my social media to private, he did send me a request on IG." Sabina smiled at the thought.

"Eric? Wow, well at least you can stay in touch with him."

"Yeah. I haven't posted anything in months. Jon was trying to make me delete everything." She shook her head. "What about you and Brandon? How are you guys?"

"It's weird. Brandon is trying to act like everything is normal, but it feels like there's so much tension between us, it's smothering. I know he's hurting."

"I think it's going to take a while before you both feel normal again, but you will."

"I know."

"You didn't tell your mom?"

"No. It would break her heart. She didn't even know I was pregnant anyway. And I think I want this to stay between us."

She put her arm around me. "I understand. I was kinda looking forward to being a godmother."

"You know, I didn't want the baby, but now I can't stop thinking 'what if.'"

"It just wasn't meant to be. God took her home for a reason."

I looked at her curiously. "Her? How do you know it wasn't a boy?"

"I had a feeling it would be a girl. Sorry, you said you didn't want to talk about it."

"It's okay. What was her name?"

She grinned. "Zoë."

I smiled back at her. "That's beautiful."

Brandon arrived home from work and saw us talking. The energy between us was still awkward. He was trying to change that, and admittedly, I needed to as well.

"Hey, B," Sabina acknowledged him.

"Hey." He looked at me and smiled. We exchanged a nonverbal hello, and Sabina could feel the shift in the energy in the room.

"Well, I'm going to start dinner." Sabina gave me a kiss on the cheek, got up, and headed toward the kitchen.

"Brandon, I need to talk to you."

"I need to talk to you too." He took her place on the couch next to me.

"I know I've been emotionally shut off, and I'm sorry."

"No need to apologize. You needed time. This was a . . . big one."

"How do you feel?"

"I've had so many mixed emotions. It's hard to process it all."

"Do you hate me?" I looked at him.

Brandon took my hand and looked into my eyes. "No. Why would you even say that?"

"You know I didn't want the baby. I feel like . . . it's my fault. Maybe if I—"

"I'ma stop you right there. This is not your fault. It never was. Things happen that are out of our control, and this was one of them. I never will hold you responsible for that."

"I feel so guilty. Maybe if I . . . wanted to have a baby, maybe then I wouldn't have lost it."

His facial expression said it all. He kissed me softly and wrapped his arms around me. It was then I knew I wasn't alone.

Chapter Thirty-six

One Wish

Nia Scott

My life was slowly returning to normal. Brandon and I had been very open with each other about the miscarriage. Tomorrow was Brandon's birthday, so I wanted to make it special for him. I told Sabina to invite the guy who asked her out. More like I had to twist her arm. Even though the police hadn't been successful in locating Jon, I reminded her that she couldn't let him continue to intimidate her and she had to move on with her life.

I should have taken my own advice. Brandon and I hadn't made love since the miscarriage. Sex was the furthest thing from our minds, but lately it had been on mine. I missed his touch. It'd been a few weeks since we'd had any intimacy with each other. I wanted to tell him it was all right to touch me like that.

Life at the hospital was back to normal as well. Dr. Haugabrook really hadn't said anything to me since I'd returned. I took that as a good thing. It was one thing to be professional, but it was another to be an ass and a borderline racist. I wasn't the type to call every white person that, but this man checked all the boxes of one. What was it with old white men with bad hairpieces in this country?

The good news was that Jayla, Anthony, and I had become a great team. They'd been empathetic to me since my miscarriage, making sure I was okay, especially Jayla. I had one patient today whose situation hit close to home, a 16-year-old girl named Megan Simpson who came in with stomach pains and thought she could be pregnant. She was a cute girl with a cinnamon complexion. She had a long black weave that fell to the middle of her back.

"I wanna have a cute baby," she told me happily as I examined her.

I pushed on her upper stomach to feel around, and she winced in pain. While I waited for her urine results, I called for a radiology tech to do an ultrasound because I did hear something upon my exam. She looked on in awe as the tech moved the wand over her abdomen. I stared at her curiously after the tech left. "Do you think you're ready for a baby?"

"Yeah, I can handle it, and my boyfriend wants me to."

I began charting. "Okay, what about your parents?"

She shrugged.

"How long have you and your boyfriend been having sex?"

"For about a year."

"Have you been using protection?"

"Sometimes."

That meant no.

"Megan, you know you're putting yourself at risk for more than just a baby by having unprotected sex."

"I'm the only one he's having sex with."

I nodded. "Okay."

"My boyfriend will help me."

"And how old is he?"

"Seventeen, but he has a part-time job."

I wanted to scream at her and talk some common sense into her as if I were her mother.

"He's going to go full-time this summer, and I know he'll take care of us."

I took it back. I wanted to slap the shit out of her.

"Do you want to go to college?"

"Yeah."

"So you want to have a baby, you're sixteen, and you want to go to college. Do you have a plan?" She didn't say anything to me, but her eyes said it all. "Let me see if your results are back." I looked in her chart. "I'll be right back."

I noticed the joy she had seemed to have diminished.

"Here." I handed her a pack of condoms once I returned. "If you're going to have sex, make him use these. Or better yet, tell him you're not ready to. If he loves you, and I mean really loves you, he'll wait."

She nodded. "Okay."

"Oh, and your test results were negative. You just have a bad case of indigestion." I handed her a few samples of antacids. "You should feel better after taking these."

A smile spread across her face. "Thank you."

I hoped she would listen to me. I could tell by the look on her face that she was relieved she wasn't pregnant. *"I wanna have a cute baby?" What kind of stupid-ass reason is that to bring a child into the world with no means to take care of it? There are so many people in this world who can't have children who deserve to. She'd better learn how to make up her own mind instead of letting her boyfriend think and make decisions for her and her body.*

The next day, Sabina and I were putting up the decorations for Brandon's birthday party. One of his friends took him out to see one of the Marvel films. I was kind of jealous because I wanted to see it as well.

Sabina was taping red streamers to the wall. "So you're doing a little party here and then going out for drinks later?"

"Yeah, it's been a while since we been out as a couple."

She smiled. "That'll be good for both of you."

"Did you invite Eric?"

The smile on her face got wider. She was damn near glowing. "Yeah, he's coming."

"Like I had to ask with that big-ass grin on your face."

"Well, I thought I should take a chance and see what happens."

"Did you tell him about Jon?"

"Yeah, he says he don't care and that if he comes around me when he's there, he'll fuck him up."

"I like him already."

Later that night, a few of Brandon's coworkers and some of his frat brothers from college arrived, and I had Jay-Z and Beyoncé setting the mood for tonight's celebration. Our home was filled with laughter and dancing.

"Yo, Brandon, you remember that one season when you tried to play football?" Jason, one of his frat brothers, reminded him. "This fool used to get the shakes every time he got a scratch playing football!"

Brandon extended his middle finger. "Shut up. I know what you're referring to, and I had a gash on my arm that was bleeding every-damn-where."

Jason grinned. "Semantics." He looked at me. "Anyway, I'm glad you didn't let that pretty lady right there get away."

"I never will, so don't get any ideas."

"Me? I would never think of coming between you and such a beautiful, intelligent woman who's clearly out of your league. I mean, what are the odds that someone so fine, so delectable, would slip by a handsome chocolate brother like myself? It's just astronomical. Yet here we are."

I shook my head. "Thanks, Jay. You're just as smooth as ever."

I gave Brandon a big kiss, then strolled over to Sabina and saw her with her friend, Eric. Wow, he was fine. He was certainly better looking than that psycho Jon. Tall, dark, handsome brother with a nice dark beard, low-cut fade, and pretty brown eyes. Sabina definitely leveled up.

"Hello? How are you all doing tonight?"

Sabina gave me a smile. "Eric, this is my girl, Nia. The one I told you about."

He spoke in a deep, sexy tone. "Hey, nice to meet you. You have such a lovely house."

He shook my hand. He had big hands, and I noticed his even bigger feet. I hoped for Sabina's sake that what they said was true.

"Thank you."

"I hear I have you to thank for convincing Sabina to see me outside of work," Eric said with a smile.

I grinned at her. "I'll take all the credit for this."

"Oh, my God."

Eric smiled. "Well, I owe you one."

I really liked this guy already. I glanced at the clock on the wall and decided now was the perfect time to toast my man. I made my way to the front of the room and got everybody's attention.

"Excuse me, everybody, but it's time for the birthday boy to blow out the candles."

I walked into the kitchen and brought out his cake and placed it on the table. Brandon was smiling at me as everyone began to sing "Happy Birthday."

"Make a wish."

He looked at me. "My wish already came true."

Brandon closed his eyes and blew out the candles. I made a wish as well and hoped it would come true.

"Stop trying to be so damn romantic," Jason yelled.

"Oh, you mean like this?"

Brandon sauntered toward me, grabbed two handfuls of my booty, and put his tongue in my mouth. The crowd showered us with oohs and aahs.

Jason laughed. "Okay, all right, I'm jealous."

After our guests left, we went to the Gold Room. It'd been a while since we went out, and I wanted Brandon to have a good time. The DJ was banging out classic nineties hip-hop and R&B from Biggie and DMX to Aaliyah. Then the crowd exploded with energy when Bell Biv Devoe's "Poison" came on. Sabina and Eric were with us, too, and from what I could see, it looked like they were really getting into each other. The club was packed with people from wall to wall.

Before we left home, I changed into a white tight dress and Manolo Blahnik stilettos. The dress had an open cut to the small of my back, and I wore a G-string underneath. When the light hit me right, it left nothing to the imagination. Being so revealing in the club was normally not my style, but I wanted to show Brandon what he'd been missing since the miscarriage, and from the way his erection was feeling against my butt, he knew, too.

Brandon wasn't the only one on hard. I could feel the eyes of almost every guy in the club on me as I ground on Brandon. I felt sexy. I hadn't felt that way in a long time.

We left Sabina in the club with Eric. She looked like she was having a good time with him. Hopefully he would be able to give her some much-needed joy and peace in her life.

Brandon and I were both feeling some type of way and needed to get somewhere alone. We didn't even make it out of the car before we started kissing and touching on each other.

"What are you doing, baby?" I asked.

"What does it look like I'm doing?"

His hand was sliding up my thigh and found the heat between my legs. A moan escaped my lips as I leaned back on the passenger side of the car.

Brandon slid the strap off my shoulder, slipped my right nipple into his mouth, and sucked it. I came on his fingers. I was so horny. I hadn't felt like this in a while. We were like some horny teenagers making out in a car. We finally made it home and got down to business. Tonight wasn't about making love. Tonight we wanted to fuck each other's brains out. I thought we'd lost that type of passion for each other, and I was tired of Brandon treating me like a delicate flower instead of a woman. Well, he certainly got over it and under my G-string. It took about three minutes to get this dress on and looking right, and Brandon had it off in three seconds. Face down, ass up: that was the way Brandon tore me up! He was like a beast the way he manhandled me into whatever position he wanted me. Front. Back. Side to side.

"Aaahhh . . . Shit . . . Don't stop . . . Oh God!"

"You like that?"

"Yes!"

He teased, "You sure you mean it?"

I yelled, "Oh, shut up and fuck me! Oh God!"

It was a good thing Sabina wasn't home yet or she would have thought Brandon was killing me the way I was moaning. I was normally not a loud person, but tonight I was on some other shit. Brandon found all my magic spots and was knocking the bottom out of all of them. He picked me up and carried me to the wall. I wrapped my legs around his body like we were in a WWE match.

We hadn't had sex like this in years. I felt wetness all around me. Each one of his thrusts was wicked and delightful at the same time. We were making the picture frames on our bedroom walls shake. After a few minutes, he took me back to the bed. Tonight was his birthday, and I was the cake. He flipped me over like a pancake and ate me like syrup was dripping. His tongue swirled around

my clit, and my legs trembled uncontrollably. I can't remember how many times I came.

I slept really good after we got done, and I woke up
in Brandon's arms feeling like a brand new woman. As
I glanced around the bedroom, I saw our clothes spread
out across the room like a tornado came through. My
G-string was draped like a teepee on the lampshade.

I smiled at him. "Hey, stranger, you know, my fiancé is
coming home any minute now."

"Really? Maybe I should go hide in the closet."

"Okay, R. Kelly."

We both laughed.

"Did you enjoy your birthday?"

"Oh, yes, I did, over and over and over again. I got my
wish all right, and I plan on getting it again."

I kissed him. "By all means, take it as much as you like!"

Chapter Thirty-seven

I Can Just Kill a Man

Nia Scott

Spring was definitely in the air. The birds were singing, and the flowers were blooming. Brandon and I were crazy in love, and Sabina was falling in love with Eric. She talked about him constantly. Since the night of Brandon's birthday, they were together every other night. Sabina was completely healed from her physical injuries, but my concern was her mental scars. I'd seen Sabina in so-called love before, but this time was different. I could tell Eric was really a good dude, and the difference in Sabina made me smile. I could tell she was thinking about her future and saw he only wanted the best for her.

I was in the kitchen making myself a grilled cheese sandwich like my dad taught me to when I was a little girl. Sabina came in and sat at the table. I noticed the grin on her face.

"What's got you cheesing? Or should I say who?"

She chuckled. "Eric is coming by tonight, and we're going to the movies later."

"Why did I know that already? You two are like joined at the hip these days."

She sighed. "I wish we were joined at the hip."

My eyebrow arched. "What? You mean you two haven't done the nasty, slapped bellies, or exchanged screw faces yet?"

"Nope. None of the above."

"Wow."

She twisted her lips. "You don't have to sound so shocked ya know."

"Sorry, I just thought with the time you two spend together . . ." I paused. "Well, come on, Sabina, you a bit of a ho," I joked.

She busted out laughing. "Shut the hell up! You a ho! I heard you the other night! 'Hit it harder, daddy! Take it, baby! Take it! Ah, ah, ah. Oh, shit!'"

My mind flashed back to that night, and she was right, and we both laughed.

"So what? It's my damn house! Anyway, you're really taking your time with him, huh?"

"Yeah. I want to make sure this time. I mean, I jumped into bed with Jon so quickly, and I didn't get a chance to really get to know him. I don't want to make the same mistake again, and Eric is okay with it."

"That's good. I'm glad he's understanding."

"Don't get it twisted. It's hard. He's so damn fine! Girl, there are times we get so deep into it. I've been taking cold showers, praying, or whatever it takes to not go there with him. Then hearing you two didn't help matters."

I smirked. "Payback is a bitch! Remember all those times in college I had to listen to you bumping and grinding all night? So there!"

"Whatever!" She pouted. "I don't miss sex. I miss really good sex."

"Aww . . . sorry, but I can't relate. Sorry for ya!"

"God don't like ugly! Heifer."

***

The next day, after I got off work, I checked my voice-mail and saw that my mother had left me five messages to call her so we could talk about the wedding. I figured I'd call her tonight and talk about it since Brandon would be out with his friend. I'd been avoiding her calls for a while now. She wanted to make this a big thing like I was Meghan Markle or somebody, but I knew I wanted something simple.

"Mom, we're not having the wedding in Chicago."

"Why not? All your family is up here."

"Because Brandon's family lives in Stone Mountain, and we live in Atlanta. Anybody who wants to come can fly down here."

"Nia, are you sure? I always pictured you getting married at New Gospel."

I sighed. "No, that's not what I want."

"All right, but you gotta pick a date so I can tell the rest of the family."

"Well, I was thinking we could do it in May of next year."

"Okay, well, that gives us plenty of time. Have you thought about a caterer yet?"

I laughed. "No, not really."

"Well, your father and I decided on Caribbean food."

My eyebrows crunched. "What do you mean you and Dad decided? For what?"

"Oh, I didn't tell you yet, but your father and I are getting married again."

I didn't say anything right away, and we both sat in silence. I could tell she was nervous to tell me. Before I knew they were seeing each other again, I would have had a lot of mixed feelings, but I did want to see them happy. Why not together?

"When is it?"

"We set the date for November tenth."

"I'll put a request in for time off, and we'll be there."

"Thank you, Nia." I could hear the smile in her voice.

I guessed there came a time when you had to let go of the past and look toward the future. The rest of our conversation went smoothly, and she even asked me to be her maid of honor. Of course, I accepted, and Sean was going to be my dad's best man.

After I got off the phone with her, I went downstairs to the kitchen to get a drink. The lights were dim, and the streetlight lit the room. I spotted broken glass on the floor, and the back door to the kitchen was open. I turned around and saw Jon holding a gun, and he had Sabina in a headlock. I'd never felt dread in my heart like I did at that moment. *I guess the past doesn't let go so easily.*

His face was scarred from our last encounter. "Hey, bitch, remember me?"

"Oh, my God! Please let her go."

I could see terror on her face. Sabina was shaking, and tears were streaming down her face.

He sniffed her hair and spoke directly into her ear. "Oh, she's fine, isn't that right, baby?" He looked at me. "Where's Brandon?"

"He's at work," I lied. "What do you want?"

"Her. She ruined my life."

"What? You ruined your own life!"

He pointed the gun at me. "Shut your fucking mouth before I blow your pretty little head off! Get over there by her!"

Jon shoved Sabina toward me. I stood in front of her, shielding her from his crazy ass.

He glared at me. "You filled her head with all that bullshit about leaving me and forced me to—"

"Forced you to what? Beat her? You beat up women."

He backhanded me across my face, sending me to the floor. Sabina screamed.

"I told you to shut up, bitch. Plus, I owe you for that shit you did to my face!"

I should have cut his throat. Sabina rushed to my side and made sure I was okay, then looked at him.

"Jon, do what you want to me, but leave Nia alone. Please."

An evil grin widened across his face, and he walked toward us. "Oh, baby, I'm gonna have so much fun with both of your asses." Jon took the barrel of the gun and rubbed it over my breasts. "Yeah, we going to have a good time, bitch. My first piece of dark meat."

I was more pissed off than afraid. This sick asshole unzipped his pants and pulled out a half-erect penis and glared at me.

"Suck it!"

He pointed the gun in my face. My common sense was telling me to obey his command, but my pride wouldn't let me do it. An annoyed expression covered his face. He grabbed me by the neck and forced me to my knees, and his nasty-ass dick was inches away from me.

"Go on."

I closed my eyes and opened my mouth, but then Sabina did the unexpected. She jumped in front of me and got down on her knees. "No, I want it first."

She grabbed his penis and rubbed it up and down, making it grow in her hands. Jon groaned with pleasure. "Yeah? You miss this cock, huh? You always did suck a mean one. Go ahead. Take notes, Nia. You're next."

Sabina spat on it and lubed him up. I was in a state of shock seeing her do this so willingly. Jon closed his eyes, enjoying the sensation. Sabina's eyes narrowed, and then her face morphed into an evil scowl as she made a fist.

I had no idea what it felt like for a man to get hit in his balls, but judging by the bitch-ass scream that bellowed from Jon, the shit must've stung a bit. He deserved to feel every one of those knuckles.

Instantly, he dropped the gun, and I scrambled toward it. He pushed Sabina away from him and staggered toward me. I never fired a gun in my life. I pulled the trigger, but nothing happened. I pulled again, and there was nothing.

"Dumb bitch!" Jon laughed and tried to charge at me, but all of a sudden, Brandon rushed in and punched Jon in the head, sending him down to the floor.

"Muthafucka, you're dead!"

Brandon pounced on him and rained down blow after blow on him. The snaps, crackles, and pops I heard resulted in busted lips, a broken nose, and other contusions. Blood squirted from Jon's nose like a tomato. Revenge was in Brandon's eyes. I placed the gun down and grabbed him before he killed Jon.

"Brandon, stop. He's down! It's over."

But it wasn't over for Sabina. She picked up his gun and stood over him, pointing it at his head.

"Sabina?"

She stared at Jon, ready to kill. "Who's the bitch now?"

"Sabina, don't do it. Please, he's not worth it."

"You fucking piece of shit! You don't deserve to live! Fuck you!"

I'd never seen the look that was in her eyes. There was a darkness that scared me. Obviously, Sabina knew how to use a gun, because she flipped the small switch on the side, taking the safety off. Her finger eased down on the trigger. Jon cowered on the floor with his pants down around his thighs, his booty out, scared to death. He released his fear and bladder on the floor.

I took a step toward her. "Sabina, don't let him ruin your life."

She trembled with anger, but then slowly lowered the gun.

"It's over," Brandon assured her.

Then this dumbass did the stupidest thing he could do and grabbed her arm, thinking he could take the gun from her. He was wrong. Thunder exploded in the room. Kyle killing himself in front of me flashed before my very eyes. All those traumatic memories rushed back to me in less than a second. Jon fell back to the floor with a gunshot wound in his chest, blood staining his shirt. Sabina stood there, unflinching, and glared at him. There was no emotion on her face. She turned and laid the gun down on the counter and walked away.

Brandon called 911.

I grabbed some kitchen towels and tried to stop his bleeding, not because I cared, but because I didn't want this fool's blood staining my kitchen floor.

Chapter Thirty-eight

How Sabina Got Her Groove Back

Nia Scott

After what went down with Jon, everybody felt a sigh of relief. Luckily for him the gunshot wound wasn't fatal. I was told that the only reason he didn't die was because he was shot with a small-caliber bullet from a .22. The bullet simply embedded itself in his chest wall and never entered the chest cavity. The police and our attorney told us that Jon would be facing charges of aggravated battery, assault with a firearm, breaking and entering, and attempted rape. He was looking at decades of incarceration. After a painful recovery from his gunshot wound, the next thing Jon had to look forward to was being someone's bitch on his cellblock.

Sabina became withdrawn after she shot Jon, and Eric came by every day, but she didn't want to see him. I knew she was trying to push him away. I understood that nearly killing a person could mess with your psyche, but I wanted to talk to her to see where her mind was at with him.

I went to her room, stood in the doorway, and saw her on her phone, scrolling away.

"What are you doing this weekend?" I asked.

"Nothing. I'm just gonna chill here."

"What about Eric? Aren't you going to see him?"

"I told him I need some space."

I walked in and sat on her bed. "Why?"

She put her phone down. "Nia, after everything that happened, I don't think I need to be dating right now."

"So you just going to throw it all away? Sabina, you haven't seen him in weeks. Now he's a good man, but he isn't going to wait forever, and I know you're crazy about him."

"Yeah, but I don't know. What if this doesn't work out?"

"Wow, this is a first. You're skipping the whole relationship phase and heading right for the breakup? Don't be like me."

"What do you mean don't be like you?" She looked at me.

"After Kyle's suicide, I pushed everybody away, including Brandon. I went back to Chicago and hid from everything. I didn't want to deal with the emotions I was feeling. Thank God Brandon didn't give up on me, and I don't want to see you give up on Eric."

"Nia, I just don't want to make another mistake."

"Have you taken your time to get to know him?"

She nodded. "Yes."

"Do you like him?"

"Yeah, I do."

"Isn't he fine?"

"Yeah, he is." She giggled. "Okay, I'm going to call him." I gave her a hug. "Good."

Sabina Singh

I couldn't believe I let Nia talk me into calling Eric. He was so happy to hear from me. After a brief conversation, he said he would come over this evening and take me out. That gave me enough time to shower and find something to wear. Honestly, hearing how happy he was made me feel really good because I'd never heard that type of excitement from a man before.

The past month had been crazy. I shot Jon. Truth was, I wanted to kill him, and I should've. If Nia weren't there, I probably would've.

Thoughts like that made me wonder if I was damaged for life. Why did Eric want to be with me after all of this? Did he just want to fuck and run? He was so nice and affectionate toward me. I'd had men treat me like that before without their own agenda. I wondered if he was truly different. I guessed there was only one way to find out.

I was looking through my clothes, trying to decide what to wear. I wasn't pleased with anything I saw. I went to Nia and told her I had nothing to wear and was going to cancel my date. She could see how nervous I was and reassured me that going out tonight would be good for me. She took me to her bedroom closet and pulled out a few sexy items to wear. After a few minutes of trying on a few outfits, I decided to wear a black skirt and blouse with some black stilettoes.

A few hours later the doorbell rang, and butterflies flew around in my stomach. I reminded myself that this wasn't the first time I'd gone out with him, but it sure felt like it. I heard Nia open the door, and his sexy voice followed.

"Hello, Nia."

"Hey, Eric, come in. Sabina, Eric's here."

Okay, showtime. I walked out of my room and saw Eric looking like he'd just stepped off a movie set with his handsome self. He had on a pair of dark blue jeans, a button-down red shirt, and a pair of Adidas.

"Hi." I smiled at him.

He greeted me with a hug. "Hey, pretty lady. It's really good to see you again."

I blushed.

"You two have fun tonight."

Eric looked at her. "See you later, Nia."

When Eric turned his back, Nia looked at me and pumped her hips forward, I guessed telling me to get some tonight. *I can't stand her!*

Eric took me to Kiku Japanese Steak House & Sushi. I ordered the shrimp platter, and he got the white fish. I always enjoyed myself when I was with him. The last time we saw each other, I almost invited him in. Then I came to my senses and stuck to the promise I made to myself— no more meaningless sex.

"How are you?" He looked in my eyes and extended his hands toward mine.

I took a sip of my drink. "I'm okay, I guess."

"I'm sorry. I'm sure you don't want to talk about it."

I took his hands. "No, it's okay. I . . . I don't mind talking about it, but I don't want to talk about it tonight."

He smiled. "That's fine with me."

"Eric, can I ask you a question?"

"Sure, what do you want to know?"

"Why me? Why are you even interested in a girl like me? I mean, you know what I've just gone through."

"I don't scare easily. Plus, I've wanted to talk to you since the first day I saw you. I think you're not only incredibly beautiful, but you're also a genuinely good woman who I want to get to know better. These past few months have been incredible. You're smart and funny, and despite everything going on in your life, you push on. You're a superwoman."

"Oh, wow, thank you. I've never had a man say that about me." I sighed. "I know you're probably wondering why we haven't gone any further."

"Not really. You've been through a lot of bullshit, so whatever time you need, you got. I'm not trying to smash." He chuckled. "I mean, I do really like you, and I wouldn't turn it down if you wanted to, but there's more to you that I really like than that."

"Well, that's good to know, but I know there are other girls out there you can be with."

He smiled. "And if that's all I wanted, I wouldn't be here with you."

I was used to men saying what they thought I wanted to hear in order to get what they wanted, but when I gazed into Eric's eyes, something inside of me believed him.

After we finished dinner, he drove back to Nia's house. Eric reached over and held my hand for the entire drive. I felt so safe with him and really didn't want this night to end. While we were driving, I decided to be bold. I opened my legs and slid his hand up my thigh. Eric was so surprised he almost lost control of the car. I gazed over at him and grinned. He smiled back at me and began to gently massage my thigh. I closed my eyes and let my mind run free. It felt so good. I reached over and touched the bulge in Eric's pants, and my God, it felt like a steel pipe in there! By the time we pulled up at home, I was ready.

"Do you want to come inside?" I asked when he parked.

"Yeah." He nodded. "Are you sure?"

In my head, I said, *you goddamn right I'm sure.* "Yeah, I am."

We went inside the house and crept through to my room. I quietly closed the door, then turned and looked at Eric. We stared at each other for a second with hungry eyes, and then he stepped toward me and kissed my lips. As I felt my other lips get moist, I slowly unbuttoned his shirt and rubbed my hands up and down his muscular chest. He lifted my blouse over my head, and I unfastened my skirt, letting it drop to the floor. I stood in front of Eric in my bra and panties, but most of all, vulnerable. His eyes studied my body as if he was making mental notes on what he was going to do. He caressed the swell of my breasts, then with one hand, unclasped my bra. Then he took one of my breasts in his mouth while his hands grasped my ass and lifted me off the floor. I was so aroused as he laid me down on my bed. He unzipped his pants. When I saw his long brown manhood, I smiled and used both of my hands to caress it up and down.

I didn't think Eric was ready for the way I was going to put it on him, but honestly, I wasn't ready for everything he had in store for me. We went through every position in the book, and I thought we invented a couple of new ones. The way he made love to me made me lose control. My moans were so loud that I didn't care who heard me. I had to let it out. I came over and over again. He held me tight in his arms as I caressed his spine with my fingertips. I couldn't help but smile with satisfaction. We fell asleep in each other's arms. *I have to send Nia a thank-you card or something for this one.*

Chapter Thirty-nine

Collision

Nia Scott

I thought a small earthquake hit us last night. Poor Eric probably didn't know what hit him. From what I heard, Sabina didn't know either, but I did know my girl handled her business. I was sure she had to sleep in after her festivities. I made a quick breakfast for myself and Brandon, and then headed off for my follow-up visit with my ob-gyn, Dr. Berman.

I took the day off from work. I was looking forward to working with Jayla and Anthony, even though Dr. Haugabrook was still trying to undermine their efforts. I swore that man had almost no redeemable qualities whatsoever. God bless the dead, but even Martin Luther King Jr. would have swung on him.

The morning traffic in Atlanta was as ridiculous as ever. Driving down five lanes of traffic was like the movie *Death Race* without the machine guns. Luckily it was flowing, but I spotted a black car speeding up behind me, zipping between lanes, and within seconds it was behind me.

"Oh, shit! You son of a bitch!" I screamed.

The car sped up, zipped around, and cut me off, tapping my front bumper. The impact made me swerve. I bumped my head against the steering wheel when I mashed the brakes.

It hurt like hell.

My car was dinged up pretty good on the right side, but the other person lost control of their car and rammed the car in front of me. I sat for a second trying to gather my bearings, hoping I wouldn't get hit by another car. I stared at the other vehicle, and nobody was moving. The driver was hurt. I opened my car door and ran over to see if they were okay.

The door was ajar, so I flung it open. "Are you . . . Oh, my God!" I couldn't believe who it was. "Robert?"

My adrenalin rushed and eased my pain, and after a quick visual assessment, I checked his vitals and noticed he wasn't breathing.

Another driver came up behind me. "Is everything okay, miss?"

"No, he's not breathing. Call the paramedics!"

Dr. Haugabrook was unconscious and looked like his windpipe was crushed. He was going to suffocate if I didn't do something quick.

More bystanders gathered behind me.

"Does anyone have a knife?" I yelled out.

"Yeah, I do!" A young Black woman stepped forward and handed me a pocketknife. I took a pen out of my jacket and cut off the back of it to make it hollow.

"What are you going to do?" she asked.

I looked at her. "I'm an emergency medicine doctor. He's not breathing. I need to put a trach in so he can breathe."

I used the knife to make a small opening in his neck, then inserted the pen directly into the trachea. He hadn't been getting any air into his lungs, so I placed my mouth on the other side of the pen and blew into it. No matter how much I didn't like him, I refused to let him die.

For about ten minutes I was breathing for him until the paramedics finally arrived on the scene. I followed the ambulance in my car to Grady.

Once we arrived, Dr. DeJesus took over. Robert regained consciousness, and they put a proper trach in.

Dr. DeJesus stared at me. "What you did was risky, but it worked. Looks like he's going to owe you for life."

I grinned and touched my head. "I guess so."

"Are you all right?"

"Ah, yeah. I just banged my head against the steering wheel."

She examined me. "Your pupils aren't dilated, and they are responding to light. You're going to be okay."

Piedmont Healthcare, Midtown Atlanta

After I left the ER, I went and saw Dr. Berman, my ob-gyn, for a follow-up visit. I'd been seeing him since the miscarriage. About a half hour later, Dr. Berman returned to the room with a funny look on his face.

"Is everything all right?"

"Yes, you're in good condition. However, your blood test did come back positive." He paused for a moment. "Nia, you're pregnant."

"I'm pregnant?"

He smiled. "Yes. Pregnant."

I touched my stomach in disbelief and sat there, blown away by what he just said to me. Tears of joy started to roll down my face. I felt like I'd been given a second chance. *Brandon is going to be so happy.*

I went home after my appointment and called Brandon to tell him what happened this morning with the car accident and Dr. Haugabrook. He was proud of me but pissed off my life was put in danger yet again. I didn't tell him the news yet. I wanted to wait until he got home.

I walked into the spare bedroom and pictured it being the baby's room. I couldn't believe it. I didn't think I wanted to be a mother until I had a miscarriage. I immediately made an appointment to see Dr. Berman next week for another checkup. I was not taking any chances this time. Brandon returned home a few hours later, and I was so excited I couldn't wait to tell him the news.

"Hey, baby, you okay?" Brandon asked after he walked through the door.

"I'm fine, baby."

He sat with me on the couch. "How's your head?"

"It's better."

"How's Dr. Haugabrook doing, and when can we sue his ass?"

I chuckled. "Oh, he's going to be fine. He won't be able to talk much for a couple of weeks, but that's just a bonus. Lawsuit pending."

"Good. Did you call the insurance company about the car?"

"Yeah, an adjuster will be coming by later to look at it."

"Okay. Man, you were like a real pro out there today. Doing an emergency tracheostomy in the middle of rush-hour traffic is crazy! What did the—"

I cut him off. "Brandon, I got something to tell you."

"Okay. What?"

"Do you think we should wallpaper the spare bedroom with Winnie the Pooh or Spiderman?"

A totally baffled expression was on Brandon's face. "What?"

"I mean, what kind of design should we do for the baby?"

Brandon gazed at me, still confused, but then what I said started to sink in. "Did you say 'baby'?"

I nodded my head and smiled.

"Oh, my God!" Brandon touched my stomach, and tears started to form in his eyes.

"I found out today at my checkup."

He hugged me and kissed me. Then he got on his knees and kissed my stomach. My eyes started to fill with tears.

He looked up at me. "To answer your question . . . Spiderman."

I started to giggle, and Brandon wrapped his arms around me.

Later that day, Sabina came in with Eric, and they saw us in the kitchen. Actually, we saw them trying to sneak by to her room. I guessed she was still getting her groove back.

She smiled nervously. "Hey, guys, wus up?"

Eric waved. "Hey, y'all."

We smiled at them.

Sabina looked around the room. "Are you guys all right?"

I grinned at her. "Hey, do you still feel like being a god-mother?"

Sabina's face dropped, then she snorted with joy. Sabina ran over and hugged me. "Yess! Oh, my God, Nia!"

Eric shook Brandon's hand. "Congratulations."

"Thank you."

She hugged Brandon as well. "I'm so happy for you both!"

"I am too. I'm still in shock."

She beamed with joy. "Well, you know I'm going to spoil the hell out of her!"

Brandon gave her the side-eye. "How do you know it's a girl?"

"I know these things," Sabina replied confidently.

We spent a good hour talking about the baby. I could tell Eric was being patient, but he had other things on his mind. I nudged Sabina, reminding her that she had a man to look after. She nodded, and they excused them-selves to her room. I FaceTimed my mom and told her.

She was bouncing up and down with joy. I even called Sean on the road and told him the news, and he was happy, claiming it was about time.

They say everything happens for a reason, right? Dr. Haugabrook ran into me for a reason. If I hadn't been on the highway, I didn't think he would still be living. Everything happens for a reason. Maybe the miscarriage was because it wasn't the right time, but now it was, and I knew Brandon would be by my side every step of the way.

Chapter Forty

Baby Girl

Nia Scott

Chicago

Five Months Later

I was well into my pregnancy, and it looked like a small volleyball in my stomach. My ankles did swell up a bit, and Brandon affectionately called them "cankles," but other than that I looked and felt good. *I'd better not have a small baby. I want her to be a big, healthy baby with fat little arms and legs you can chew on.* I couldn't believe Sabina was right about it being a girl. I was surprised she wasn't pregnant too with all the humping she and Eric had been doing.

Funny thing was my sex drive had increased since I got pregnant. Poor Brandon was worn out every day. *Sorry, baby, but momma got needs.* I was still able to keep up at the hospital, even though I planned on taking extended time off after the baby was born.

Dr. Haugabrook didn't really say anything nasty to me anymore. He even thanked me for saving his life. I relished his humbleness.

We flew out to Chicago for my parents' wedding. I never thought I would see this day.

My mother looked beautiful, and my father couldn't stop smiling as she walked down the aisle at New Gospel. This was the wedding my mom had dreamed I would have, so it was only right it became hers. Sean looked handsome standing next to Dad. I could see a lot of cougar bridesmaids staring at him. I could already tell Sean was going to have a ball after this.

At the reception, my parents were dancing to Luther Vandross's version of "Always and Forever."

Brandon was dancing with me and looked at my parents.

"Aw, look at them. Don't they look happy?"

"Yeah. That's going to be us in twenty years, and little Zoë is going to be saying the same thing about you."

I smiled. "If I don't drive her crazy first."

"You'll be fine." He looked around. "Where's Sean?"

"Probably in between some bridesmaid's legs somewhere."

"That sounds about right. Are you hungry?"

"Yeah. Zoë and I need some cake."

"I got ya."

Brandon rubbed my belly and made his way to the table as I walked over and had a seat. My cankles were getting at me, and Zoë was being acrobatic. Brandon brought my cake, and I inhaled it. A few minutes later, my father came over to me.

"Baby girl, may I have this dance with you and my grandbaby-to-be?"

I smiled. "Yes, you may."

As we danced together, I felt like a little girl again.

"Nia, I'm so glad you're here today. This means so much to your mother and me."

"I love you, Dad. I just want you both to be happy."

"I know, and we will be. Like I know you and Brandon will make that little bundle of joy in there happy, too."

March Fourth

I still hadn't had the baby. She was being stubborn, just like me. I was over the whole magic of being pregnant. Dr. Berman said that they would induce me in two days if I didn't have her before then. I was so ready. Brandon was out at the store picking up a few things, and Sabina was home with me. I felt fat and miserable.

I glared at my stomach. "You better bring your butt out of there, little girl."

Sabina looked at me. "Don't yell at my baby."

"Your baby? Yeah, okay, you want her?"

She snickered. "It'll be over soon, and I'll have my little Zoë to spoil."

"You can breastfeed her, too, while you're at it."

Sabina cupped her tits. "Sorry, these are for Eric only."

I got up and walked to the kitchen. "Thanks for that mental picture. I hope Brandon isn't expecting me to have another baby anytime soon because the factory will be officially closed after this."

"You know you're a damn liar. Brandon is going to be on your ass as soon as possible."

"Oh, yeah, we will be getting it in, but I'm going to have my tubes cut, burned, and thrown away."

"Are you for real?" Sabina looked mortified. "You going to do that?"

I sighed. "Nah, I don't think so, but I'm not going to be having five or six little kids running around here either. Maybe we can try for a boy in the future." I reached into the freezer and grabbed a Hot Pocket to toss in the microwave.

"Good, I wouldn't want little Zoë to be lonely."

"Well, the way Eric is humping on you all the time, she'll have a little godbrother or godsister soon enough."

"Not yet. I ain't popping any babies out of this—"

"Sabina!" I shouted.

She came toward me, almost slipping, but she braced her fall by grabbing on to the countertop. "Oh, shit! I guess your water finally broke. That's what you get for yelling at her. C'mon."

Sabina rushed me to the hospital in my car, and I called Brandon to meet us there. The contractions were like menstrual cramps times a hundred. We got to the hospital, and I was rushed to labor and delivery.

"Oh God, where is Brandon?"

Sabina took my hand. "He's on his way, Nia, but I'm not leaving you."

A contraction hit me hard, and I damn near crushed her hand.

Sabina squealed, "Oh, shit! Okay, you can let my hand go now, dammit!"

Just then, Brandon came rushing into the room. "I'm here now, baby! It's going to be okay!"

"You did this to me! You horny bastard! It's your fault why I'm going through all this pain!"

"I know, baby. If I could have this baby, I would."

"Fine! Why don't you squeeze this out of your . . . Ooooooh ssssshiiiiit!"

I squeezed the shit outta Brandon's hand. "Oh, sweet mother of crap!"

"Don't let her get your hand, Brandon. It's murder."

"I want morphine! Drug me! Knock me the fuck out!" Well, let's just say this wasn't my most graceful moment. But about four hours later, which felt like a lifetime, I had a seven-pound and twenty-inch baby girl. It felt like a Volkswagen Bug popped out between my legs, but I was so overwhelmed with joy when they placed little Zoë Aaliyah Griffin in my arms that all the pain I felt went away.

"Oh, my God, Brandon, she's so beautiful."

He smiled and kissed us both. "I know. She looks just like her mother."

"I'm sorry I said those nasty things to you. That was mostly the pain talking."

"Mostly?"

I looked at my beautiful daughter and caressed her face. "I love you, Zoë. I promise not to screw your life up too much."

Four months later, we were all in a church in Atlanta with my little baby girl, Zoë. Sabina was my maid of honor and made sure I was okay while feeding Zoë. My mother and father were here along with Sean.

Brandon was a proud father. Zoë was going to be a daddy's girl just like I was. He was so protective of her I felt sorry for any boy who wanted to date her when she grew up.

I swore Sabina thought she was her baby with the way she took care of her. Sabina and Eric were still together as well. I was happy for them.

Zoë was so beautiful. I couldn't believe she came out of me. I was a mother. That was unbelievable, and I couldn't imagine my life without her now. I looked at Zoë, and she smiled at me. She was going to be just like me when she grew up. We were going to raise her to be the Black queen she was destined to be.